THE COLDWATER JOB

A Crucible of Legacy Novella

MIKE CAHOON

STAGHEART PRESS, LLC

For my grandmothers, gone too soon,
Who lived lives full of grace, humility, and love,
And taught me to do the same,
I will always miss you.

CONTENTS

Chapter One

The College

As the train of three massive wagons, each drawn by a pair of long haired Northern oxen, plowed through the weather and frozen snow, the powerful beasts strained and snorted against their harnesses. Steam plumed from their nostrils and mouths as their coats froze in matted clumps against their flanks. Bent into the wind, wrapped tightly in his sealskin coat and furs as well as a double layer of scarves, a furred cap and a hood that contained his cascade of red hair and beard, Holton Hart wondered grimly at the strangeness of mages. The journey had been long and rough, with this last leg from Baleswell being particularly unpleasant. He had spent a great deal of time soothing the beasts as best he could and encouraging them to keep their pace up despite the conditions. Now, he was more than ready to get this job over and done with.

Wind tore across the frozen tundra of the Far North in an unending, maddening gale at all hours. It howled over the low hills and scrub land, sending the ice rain cutting through the air like razor blades. It made quick work of any cloak or coat, soaking it through in moments. Even the thickest of heavy weather garments was barely a boon to a traveler in these dangerous and remote lands. But anything was better than bare flesh. The harsh environment would turn skin blue and frigid in minutes, then cause the very blood to freeze in your veins and leave you a blackened corpse in less than a day. Only the incredibly desperate, blindly brave or the deathly foolish dared to scrape out a living in the unforgiving region, which made it all the stranger that a clan of magicians called this place their home.

Beside Holton, his copilot raised an arm wrapped in a triple layer of clothing and pointed a gloved hand out into the snowfall. On the horizon, a dark shape had emerged out of the storm. At a distance, it looked like a cluster of black trees jutting up out of the frozen earth. But as they drew closer, they saw that it was a series of towers all grouped together on the north shore of a long, ice filled fjord. They stood like sentinels at the edge of the world, a final outpost of civilization, stalwart in the face of the perpetual ice and unending winter of the White Wastes. All that lay between that frozen land and this northernmost continental shore was the Coldwater Sea, a churning, treacherous ship-killer filled with great icebergs, white whales and strange monsters, if you believed the stories. And Holton had seen far too much in his lifetime to dismiss even the strangest of stories out of hand.

The wagon train's heavy, studded wheels steadily ate up the leagues as it thundered along over the snow and ice toward the great structures. By the time they reached the Coldwater Magician's College, it was nearly evening and night was rapidly pushing the remnants of light over the horizon. The dark walls loomed over them, black stone stark against the landscape of white and gray. Up close, it became clear that within the outer wall, the College was one large structure. It was a long, narrow castle with a dozen spindly towers interspersed along its length. It looked like something out of legend, an ancient place of dark magic and lost secrets. Holton could see the glow of lights through many of the windows and wondered how many mages were sequestered out here in these distant halls.

They approached the main entrance, a set of wrought iron doors that towered at least two stories high. They did not have to knock. The doors screamed as they swung inward, propelled by an unseen mechanism. There were no guards or watchers on the walls as far as Holton could see. As they passed the threshold of the outer wall, the sound of the wind was dampened down slightly by the barrier. They moved into the courtyard between the outer wall and the castle itself, which sat eerily empty. Their ox's heavy breathing and clopping hooves crunching over the icy stone was audible now. A short, broad staircase led to the great entrance way into the castle, a massive archway of black stone that surrounded another set of imposing iron doors. Above the doorway, a single banner hung with the crest of the College. It was a black, seven pointed star inverted on a white field, with its odd point facing down.

As they reined their wagons to a stop before the great entrance doors swung outward with another wail, frozen hinges shrieking in protest at being forced open. Two men stood in the doorway, swathed in dark robes. One was tall and lank, bearing a lustrous white beard and hair combination that was somewhat despoiled by the large bald patch at his crown. The other man was short, broad and as round as a barrel with a prickly growth of gray stubble spread equally across his face and head, giving the impression that he shaved the entirety of his head at the same time. Holton leapt down from the wagon and trudged up the icy steps towards them. When he spoke, his voice was muffled from the layers of cloth.

"We've got your shipment from Baleswell."

"Where is Padriack?" The shorter man demanded without ceremony, eyeing him suspiciously, "And who are you?"

"Padriack and his whole crew have come down with the White Fever. There's been an outbreak of it down south. I'm Aden, a long hauler out of Avingard. Padriack hired me and my crew to come up and make his runs while he recovers." Holton lied. He did not know if the rumors that some mages could pry into your thoughts held any truth, but as he dug about inside the layers of his jackets he prayed neither of these two were skilled in that particular discipline. He produced a rolled up piece of parchment and held it out to them, "He sent notice."

The shorter man ripped the scroll out of Holton's hands and unfurled it, eyes moving quickly while murmuring under his breath. The taller man raised an eyebrow, "The White Fever you say? We hadn't heard anything about an outbreak."

"Came on fast and hard. Burned through most of the frontier towns like a wildfire." Holton shrugged, unsure if the motion was even visible under all the layers, "Not surprised the news hasn't reached you yet, up here all alone like you are."

The shorter man snarled as he grasped the parchment in one hand and brandished it at Holton like a weapon, "Padriack knows he's meant to keep us abreast of any and all changes to the deliveries, *any and all*! This is a breach of our contract..."

Holton held up his double gloved hands, "Don't blame me. I'm just here doing the job I was hired to do."

The taller man sighed and put a hand on his companion's shoulder, "Roegan, we can deal with any issues we have with Padriack's services on his next delivery, when the man has recovered. There's no point in placing the blame at these people's feet."

The shorter man, apparently Roegan, glowered but gritted his teeth as he nodded. Then he waved and a troupe of figures clothed in heavy winter cloaks emerged from the gloom within the castle and marched past them down the stairs. It was impossible to glean much information about them, as they were so heavily wrapped in clothes that only their eyes showed from between the hoods and scarves. The rest of Holton's crew had already begun the cumbersome process of opening the frozen locks on the wagon's rear doors, so the figures were able to begin pulling crates and barrels out immediately. They worked quickly and silently, in near perfect unison, soon leaving the three wagons barren as a larder after a long winter. A few of the cloaked figures took on the task of leading the wagons away, walking them around to a side yard out of sight. The other four members of Holton's crew were left standing in the weather at the base of the stairs, shapeless and shivering even in their heavy gear. The tall man beckoned for them to follow, leading Holton and his crew through the great doors and into the depths of the black castle.

Inside, all traces of the foul weather outside immediately dropped away. They were greeted with a warm and dimly lit antechamber which was sparsely decorated but spacious, totally silent but for their shuffling coats and boot steps. The walls were lined with amber witchlights embedded in ornate iron fixtures along the walls, bathing the dark stone in a warm glow. The interior of the castle was significantly warmer than outside, as though there were a roaring hearth hidden somewhere just out of sight. After shaking the snow from their coats, Holton and his crew filed in behind the two robed men. They were led through the antechamber and into a long entrance hallway lined with carved columns and ending in a massive double staircase that curved to the second level. Holton noted that despite the hall's spartan lack of decoration, the columns bore swirling carvings of strange, eldritch beasts frozen in place as they snapped and hissed at each other. The effigies were of no creatures Holton had ever encountered, and he thanked whatever gods there might be of that good fortune. The tall man began speaking as they made their way down the long hallway towards the stairs.

"I am Nolan Felice, Steward here at the College, and this is Brent Roegan, our Castellan. We work in close cohort to manage all services for which we must deal with the world outside our gates. Since I'm sure you will be staying the night, as traveling at night in these conditions would be ill advised, we have prepared rooms in novices quarters for you."

"My crew and I appreciate your hospitality." Holton said, bobbing his head.

"Perhaps Padriack already informed you of the conditions of our hospitality," Roegan cut in as they walked, speaking gruffly, voice still carrying an unmistakable note of annoyance, "but I am going to reiterate them for you so there will be no further *misunderstandings*."

Felice sighed but Roegan plowed on with the tact of a driven bull, "You are to be confined to the novices wing for the duration of your stay here and you will be served your meals in the common area. You are not to wander the castle or the grounds for any reason. You are not to bother the novices or question them as to their studies. You are not to approach or speak to any of the students unless they engage you first. If you are found to be in breach of any of these rules, you will be expelled from our Castle and left out on the ice immediately, if you are lucky. If you're not so lucky-"

"Yes, yes, Roegan," Felice cut him off, sounding exasperated, "I believe they get the point."

"You have nothing to worry about, good sir." Holton intoned in as deferential a voice as he could muster, "We know better than to meddle in the affairs of mages. But may I ask, what of our wagons, our oxen?"

"Our people will see to the care of your beasts and your wagons." Roegan waved a dismissive hand.

"You have your own grooms and stables? Are you certain they are..."

The shorter man cut him off, turning to glare at the red haired thief over his shoulder, "Within these halls, we manipulate the arcane and wield the very essence of life itself. Do you really believe we can't handle the breakdown of a wagon train?"

"I mean no offense, my Lord, but those wagons are our livelihood..." Holton pushed on.

"We have a spacious stable yard on the northern end of the castle, Alvin." Felice cut in, giving Roegan an exasperated stare, "It is sheltered and warm and I assure you our stable master is very experienced. Your beasts and wagons will be in good hands."

Holton nodded, speaking quickly, with a look of relief on his face, "Thank you, my Lord. My team and I will rest well tonight in that knowledge."

"One last thing." The round mage turned around to stare them down once again, "Your weapons, we will be taking them for the night."

Holton nodded and looked around at the others. They all began to pull various armaments from under their cloaks and within their layers of clothing. Light crossbows, hunting knives and rusted old militia blades were dropped into a pile at the feet of the Castellan. He grunted approvingly and waved a hand. The ground groaned and split, the stones of the floor moving into small mounds letting the pile of weapons tumble into the hole. Roegan made another wave and the small chasm resealed itself, leaving a smooth floor with no sign of what had been covered up.

Holton gave the mages a grin, "Now, would you mind if we find that fire you spoke of? It has been a very long, very cold ride here."

"When are we going to make our move?" Barney was pacing the small room while fiddling with a loose string on his shirtsleeve. The young Northman's scarred face furrowed in frustration. They had been taken to their rooms in the wing of the castle where the novices were all kept cloistered together. It consisted of a large, two storied central chamber with several winding halls lined with individual rooms that extended in various directions. It bore more furnishings than the previous halls they had passed through, but just barely. Small sitting areas were formed of leather chairs and couches clustered together around simple rugs and tables. Some shelves lined the walls, packed tightly with musty old tomes and littered with scrolls and scraps of parchment, and there were a few large hearths interspersed throughout the central room that hosted piles of gently glowing rocks rather than fire.

The smattering of men and women that resided in the novices quarters had watched them curiously on their arrival, but had left them alone for the majority of the evening. They were, universally, buried in some book or scribbling away furiously with ink and pen, far too engrossed in their studies to give the newcomers more than a passing glance. Holton and his crew had all dressed down from their cold weather gear and congregated into a single room after dinner. Bellies full, they lounged around in uneasy silence. There was a slit of a window through which they could watch the steadily worsening storm as it raged silently beyond the castle walls.

Holton stood, leaning against the window ledge, watching the wind whip snow furiously past. His sister Erin sat on the bed with her eyes closed, her mop of strawberry blonde hair leaned against the wall. Beside her sat Taron, who was methodically using a bone white comb to brush out his bushy beard. The lockbreaker was grinning as he watched Barney's restless procession, a mischievous glint in his eye.

"What are you so bothered about?" He goaded the younger man, "Got somewhere you need to be? A young lady waiting for you back in Baleswell?"

Barney shot him a look as he finally tore the string loose from his sleeve and held it aloft between to fingers. There was a flash as it incinerated instantly in a tongue of light and heat.

"Gods dammit, Barney!" Holton turned from the window and growled in a low voice, "Do you not remember the wizard's instructions? None of that unless it's absolutely necessary."

"Sorry, boss." The younger man grinned sheepishly, "Won't happen again."

"See that it doesn't, or it might be all our asses." The red haired thief glared at him for a moment before looking to the final member of his crew, "Anyone out there notice that, Jarryd?"

The Oaren man had been leaning against the door, arms folded over his chest. He cracked it open and looked out into the hallway for a moment before turning back and shaking his head. His golden skin caught the amber light and made it look particularly unusual, accentuating the already marked foreignness of his almond shaped eyes and dark hair.

"Seems clear." Jarryd said in his quiet, smooth voice, "But the Fireweaver raises a fair question, Holt. We need to make our move soon."

Holton nodded, "We'll wait a bit more. I want to make sure most of the castle is asleep before we go. You heard that fat old mage, they don't take kindly to people they catch snooping about here. The Wizard said the Glass is something they won't abide losing lightly, so we'll need to move fast once we have it."

Jarryd nodded, rubbing his mustache and reclaiming his spot leaning against the door. Barney grumbled something, but threw himself into the wooden chair at the desk, the only other piece of furniture in the room, and started scratching at a splinter of wood. On every job, this was always the hard part. The waiting ate at you, gave you the itches. But it would not be long now. Holton turned back towards the window and resumed watching the snowfall. It was coming down even harder now, sheets of white falling so thick it was impossible to see anything beyond. Not long at all. Just let all these mage's get nice and deep into their dreams and it would be time.

Chapter Two

Another Locked Door

Taron had tucked his comb away and was sitting on the edge of the bed by the time Erin slipped back into the room, bundles of dirt brown novice's robes tucked under her arms. As they donned the pilfered cloaks, Erin informed them that all the novices had left the common room and turned in for the night, except for one young man who was slumbering outside in a chair. She had managed to steal the cloaks from the communal laundry at the far end of the room. His robe had a stain and smelled like onion soup but he tugged it on anyway. Barney had been practically clawing at the walls before Erin reappeared and shot to his feet when he heard the news. Holton had had to snap at him again to fall in line as they opened the door and filed out into the hallway. The kid looked like a hound with his tail tucked between his legs as he followed along, trying desperately not to look like the chastising had gutted him.

Taron knew Barney was dangerous, he had seen what the Fireweaver was capable of with his own two eyes, but it was hard to take the kid seriously when he tried so hard to look the part. He was always glaring around with his chest puffed up and making his fingers spark and smoke, like he could not wait to burn something down. Taron had found it impossible to stop teasing the young man, especially since he was so easy to rile up. The Northman grinned at the thought as they all followed

Holton through the common room, passed the sole remaining novice who was sprawled snoring in one of the chairs. They filed out into the main hallway, light on their feet and quiet as church mice.

Holton led the way, closely followed by Erin, then Barney, then himself, and finally Jarryd, stoically bringing up the rear per usual. Whenever they passed the narrow windows, they could glimpse the night outside and the worsening snowstorm still roiling around the castle. It even howled through the court-yard now, the high walls doing little to dampen it's fury. Silently, Taron wondered how bad it would get before it finally let up. Had there ever been a storm so strong it toppled a castle? A sudden noise ripped him from his revere and caused them all to stop dead in their tracks. It was the echoing of footsteps coming from somewhere deeper within the castle before them. Holton motioned and they all moved to seek cover within the alcoves of the hallways that led off the main chamber. Taron ducked into one beside Erin, both pressing themselves into the shadows and barely breathing as they waited.

Time dragged on as they listened to the footsteps getting louder and louder, seeming to fill the chamber with their unrelenting rhythm. Eventually, a group of cloaked figures marched into the main chamber, emerging from a hallway at the far end. There were a dozen figures who wore cloaks similar to the simple brown smocks of the apprentices, but of an embroidered, dark gray. None spoke nor did they pause as they passed by the hidden crew, moving with a sort of practiced discipline. Taron noted they each carried a small, dark box in their hands. The boxes appeared to be made of some sort of dark metal and were simple, inornate. He wondered at their contents, leaning out slightly to get a better look, before Erin put a hand on his chest. He gave her a look but put his back against the stone once again. As the figures approached the rear of the great hall, the massive doors screeched open once again.

The blast of cold air that exploded into the hallway carried flurries of snow and ice, peppering the dark stone with white. It pushed the heat from the great hall out all at once and made Taron's breath catch in his chest. He had to force himself not to hiss as it drove the air from his lungs. The figures barely seemed to notice. They waited in silence until the doors were fully open, then marched out into the tempest outside without hesitation. Once the last of them had crossed the threshold, the doors immediately began to shut again. The earsplitting wailing of iron on iron pierced the howling storm for several excruciating seconds before dying away as the doors came together with a resounding clashing of metal. They waited for a long moment after the figures had left before moving back out into the main area. The chamber had immediately begun to heat back up. Whatever magic kept these halls warm worked quickly. By the time they had all gathered together again, it was as though the storm was a thing of the past.

Taron looked at Holton questioningly, "What the hell was that?"

The red haired thief shook his head, "No idea. Mage's business, not ours."

"What if they're still out there when we need to make our exit?" Erin demanded. She was casting uneasy glances back and forth between the large doors and the hallway where the cloaked figures had emerged.

"We'll deal with it." Holton said, a note of finality bringing the discussion to a close.

After they regathered their wits, they quickly found their way to the kitchen. They had come here to take account of their delivery, and for the meal that followed. The kitchen was a long chamber with a half dozen hearths and a whole host of cook stations. Earlier, it had been a flurry of activity, with scores of apprentices working the bellows and seeing to the various preparation. The dining hall was a cavernous chamber adjacent to the kitchen, full of long tables and benches, as uncomfortable and spartan as the rest of the castle had proven to be. Their meal there had been a subdued affair, sitting amid the throngs of novice mages who ate under the ever-present glare of Castellan Roegan. Now the kitchens sat silent and they moved through them quickly, finding their way to the larders with ease. There, the large crates and barrels that had been their cargo now sat empty in orderly rows, waiting to be reloaded onto the wagons tomorrow.

Jarryd, Barney and Holton immediately began the process of flipping the crates upside down and prying off the false bottoms with kitchen knives and metal ladles. In no time, they had revealed the insides, which were packed with layers of wax cloth. Inside the padding were their real weapons. Holton recovered his hatchet and long knife, while Jarryd found his two short Oaren blades. While Barney and Erin each found their accoutrements of knives, Holton tossed Taron his long knives and his leather wrapped bundle of tools. Taron strapped his weapons back onto his belt and tucked the bundle inside his coat, ensuring it was secured carefully. He looked up and saw Holton pull the last item out of the secret compartment; a small charm on a necklace. It appeared to be a simple bronze compass, but with a face that curved outward like a half a glass ball. The pendant glowed with a warm light in his palm as all four hands spun lazily around, moving freely, until they suddenly all locked in a single direction. They pointed towards the heart of the castle, and slightly up. He stared at it for a moment, then tucked it inside his shirt. Once they had all been outfitted with their gear, Holton directed them out of the kitchen and back to the main hall.

They quickly found the staircase that led to the second floor. Padding up as silently as they could manage, they all kept an ear out for more unexpected residents of the castle wandering at night. More of the unnatural images engraved the banister and stairs, a mess of eyes and teeth and tentacles that looked more like nightmares than reality. They seemed almost intentionally disturbing. Taron eyed the carvings, wondering if they were works of some crazed artisan or based on something the carver had actually seen. He decided it was better that he never find out. At the top of the stairs, the hall split into three directions. The glow of the witchlights barely beat back the darkness. As they crept down the hall to the left, Taron eyed the shadowy alcoves and passages they passed with a suspicious eye, his talented hands held ready near the knives in his belt.

The ever-present grin slipped from his face a bit. He decided he was no fan of this place. It was too quiet, too still. It was like wandering through a crypt, frozen and forgotten up here at the edge of the world. They filed into a large junction where several hallways came together and formed a sort of nexus point. A sculpture on a raised dais stood silently dominating the center, forcing everyone who passed through to move around it. The image was of a scrawny, robed man with long hair, a hook nose and slumped shoulders. He stared down the main hall with a wistful look on his carved face. Taron eyed the statue, looking for a plaque or inscription, curious what sort of man deserved such an honor in this oddly barren place. On the backside, inscribed across the base, he found his answer. A tilted, flowing script read, *Quentin Cross, Founder & First Keeper of the College*.

"Not exactly the most pleasant looking fellow, is he?" He whispered back to Jarryd.

The Oaren shook his head, "Doesn't look like he would have done too well up here in the cold."

Taron considered this. He wondered vaguely what had possessed the mad bastard to build this strange school up here in the first place. It seemed like such an odd choice, even more so now that he had seen the apparently frail founder's likeness. But there was little time to dwell on it as Holton led them to another set of stairs, this one smaller and winding around blind corners. Taron realized they were climbing one of the towers. He could see the grounds getting more and more distant below as they passed each of the slotted windows. He sighed. Mages and their towers, what a horrendous cliché.

They climbed the stairs, passing more dimly lit and empty floors. Some showed only more narrow hallways while others opened up into great rooms. In these they saw the hallmarks of a school, desks and matched chairs, stacks of writing implements, chalk boards, delicate tools and implements. Walls lined with shelves of books, charts of sigils and illustrated depictions of various animals and plants and diagrams he could neither make heads nor tails of. After what seemed an eternity of climbing, they reached a landing and Holton's compass leveled out, pointing straight towards a large, metallic door nestled in a recessed archway. Taron estimated they were somewhere near the top of the tower as he looked out the narrow window into the unfathomable darkness below. Holton stuffed the compass inside his shirt and tried the door.

Unsurprisingly, it was locked. The red haired thief motioned for Taron. The lockbreaker cracked his head one way, then the other, before approaching the door. He regarded the lock with the trained eye of a professional, leaning down to examine it. It appeared to be fairly mundane, but with these damned wizards you just never knew. He rustled around in his belt pouch and pulled out a small circular disk of flat bronze. It bore a simple design, one which had always looked to Taron like a poor imitation of a snake's head. He held it up to the door only for it to immediately begin glowing with a sickly yellow light.

"Trapped." He confirmed for the others, "Can't say how, but probably nothing too friendly if I had to guess."

"Can you disarm it?" Holton pressed.

"Yes, but it'll take awhile." He cast a meaningful glance towards the stairs, "Think we'll be alright?"

Holton set his jaw, "We'll have to be. Erin, you and Jarryd go back down the stairs. Signal us if anyone's coming."

The other two nodded and moved down the winding staircase. Barney and Holton stood on the landing, ready if they should they be needed. Taron pulled out his leather tool pouch and unrolled it on the floor before him. Inside, an array of metallic instruments and disks inscribed in runes and flowing symbols were laid out and perfectly organized. He grinned affectionately down at them as they gleamed in the low light. The tools and knowledge of how to use them had cost him a fortune and nearly a decade of his life to cobble together from various two-bit magicians and shady peddlers, but all the trouble had been worth it. With these tools he was a lockbreaker the likes of which the North had never seen before. With these he had beaten more strongboxes and safe rooms than he could count. He even had broken into the vaults of the Blackwater Banking Houses, a feat some had said was impossible. His grin widened at the memory as he unbuckled a cloth lined pouch and pulled out a pair of gold rimmed, circular eyeglasses and hooked them over his ears. As soon as he did, the world lit up.

The formerly dark halls shone with an array of glowing lines and symbols which ran the walls and ringed the windows, layered on top of the far subtler glow of the stones themselves. Looking down, he could see the energy that thrummed inside his hands and the tools themselves, white hot and pulsing with life. He looked at the door and could see the spell work that ran through it like veins through a body. He took a breath and picked up a long, thin instrument like a needle with a hook at the end in one hand and a silver disk in the other. He gingerly began to adjust the first thread of energy with the needle, bending the light ever so slightly, before placing the disk on the door between it and the lock. When he let go, the disk hung on the thread like a spider. He looked over the top of his eyeglasses and saw the disk seemed to be hovering in place, no sign of the energy that it clung to. Pushing his glasses back up with his palm, he picked up another disk and went to work on the next line of light. He started to hum a jaunty tune to himself as he worked. With his tools, even these mage's locks were no match for him. After all, it was just another locked door.

It took him a while, rerouting the strands of power and locking them in place. It was delicate work, like stretching the lines of a piece of fabric in a cloth to create a hole without allowing them to rip or deform the weave. But eventually he had cleared all the lines leading to the lock away, leaving it no more complex than the door of any other castle room. He slid his lock picks inside, working the tumblers ever so gently as he chewed his tongue. He closed his eyes and listened, making minute adjustments until he was rewarded with the telltale click of the lock popping open. Grin once again breaking out across his face, he turned to look at Holton. The red haired man raised an eyebrow and he gave him a quick nod. Holton motioned to Barney and the two turned toward the door, Holton's hands drifting down to his weapons and Barney lifting his hands to a ready stance, as though he were a pit fighter preparing for a bout. Taron suppressed an urge to snort and grabbed the handle. When Holton nodded to him for the second time, he ripped the door open in one quick motion. The discs all moved with it, clinging to the door as though they were nailed in place.

Holton and Barney moved into the room together, and Taron ducked in right behind them. The room was a large semi-circle chamber which seemed to encompass most of this floor of the tower. It was a simple room, sparsely decorated with a sitting area before a large hearth on one side of the room and a massive writing desk that sat beneath a window on the opposite side. Shelves of books and scrolls lined the walls, a haphazard array of notes and tomes which even Taron's untrained eye could see held little regard for formal organization. Directly across from where they entered another door hung partially open. The three men crossed the room in a few short steps and checked the next room. It was a similarly austere bedchamber, unremarkable aside from the fact that its resident should have been present at this time of night.

"Damn," Holton cursed as he moved to turn the covers over, eyeing the empty bed with annoyance, "she's not here and neither is the Glass."

A loud cry sounded above and brought them all spinning around. Seated on one of the rafters was a massive black owl. It stared at them, globe-like eyes luminescent in the low light. They all stared at it for a moment. Then Holton snorted.

"I guess that's what the compass was tracking." He pulled out a black feather from his pocket, and tossed it to the floor, "The Wizard said this would get us to the target. Guess we'll need to figure out a new plan."

Taron scratched at his beard and bent down to double-check under the bed. He found nothing but a few errant dust bunnies taking cover beneath. Holton pressed his hand into the mattress.

"Cold."

"Doesn't mean much in this." Taron glanced toward the window. They were at the highest point in the tower and outside the storm raged against the stone. It shook the panes of glass in their frame.

"Means she's not just stepped out for the privy." Holton asserted before sighing, "We can't count on her being back anytime soon. Means we'll have to go to her."

Taron clicked his tongue. He did not like the idea of delving even deeper into this strange castle. But he took a deep breath and motioned towards Holton's chest. The thief nodded and dug inside his shirt. He pulled out the familiar domed bobble, holding the bronze base in his palm. The four hands swung around, swimming lazily through the open space as though they floated in water. Holton searched around on the bed for a moment before he found what he was looking for. He held up a single gray hair.

"Let's hope the old girl doesn't have a balding lover." Taron commented, earning a snort from Barney. Holton ignored his comment and clutched the hair in his fist.

They all watched the little hands spin around. Barney practically whispered, "Are we close enough?"

"If she's in the castle it should find her no problem." Taron told him in a low voice.

The hands finally all came together, laying over each other so well they practically melded into a single arrow pointing in one direction. They pointed straight down.

Chapter Three
Playing a Part

As the night wore on, the old tower seemed to get colder and more drafty. Erin found herself shivering against the cold, even under the apprentice's cloak. She rubbed her arms as she paced back and forth, staying near the entrance to the room. Beyond the landing at the base of the stairs, this floor of the tower was set up like a classroom, with a circle of desks and chairs that occupied the majority of the space. At first she had examined the shelves of books and scrolls that lined the walls interspersed with detailed graphs and intricately illustrated pictures. Erin tried to make some sense of these, but they depicted either the physiology's of creatures she had never seen or sciences she had no frame of reference for. It unsettled her, so she ended up avoiding them and staying near the staircase instead.

Meanwhile, Jarryd leaned against the wall with his eyes locked on the passage that wound downwards. The man seemed undisturbed by the dropping temperature and she wondered at his persistent, unshakable composure. Ever since he had joined their crew, no matter how dire the job got, he never seemed unsettled or even to worry. She thought it might have something to do with his time as a soldier in the Oarenhiem Army, but he had never been particularly forthcoming about the details of his previous life. Despite all that, he was solid as an old evergreen and fiercely loyal to her brother, so she supposed he was entitled to a bit of privacy.

Her curiosity was interrupted when a sudden noise caught her attention. There was a sound coming from somewhere below them. It was steady and rhythmic, like footsteps, but muffled and barely audible, like someone was padding around on bare feet. As though they were trying not to be heard. Erin looked to Jarryd, whose hands had already dropped to the hilts of the twin blades which peeked out from beneath his robe. Erin held up a finger for him to wait and motioned towards the staircase that led back up to where her brother and the others were working. They hurried up the stairs a bit, stopping once they were hidden from sight, and listened. The footsteps grew louder as they mounted the landing below them. Then the sound moved away, growing slightly quieter. Erin gave Jarryd a look and they slowly moved down, edging their way around the curved wall until they could peer into the classroom.

There was a figure in a black cloak moving among the desks. It rummaged around the room, seemingly looking for something. In the low light, it was hard to discern anything about the figure but Erin could vaguely make out it muttering under its breath. They watched it for a moment, tense and ready to move if it noticed them. But it was fixated on its task. It's searching became more and more frantic as it rummaged around the shelves, dropping books on the floor and rifling through scrolls and stacks of paper with little regard for their care. Jarryd tapped Erin on the shoulder and nodded back up the stairs, but she shook her head. He frowned but stayed where he was. She turned her attention back to the figure. It had slowed its search somewhere near the rear of the room. After a while, the figure stopped moving and stood still with its arms held limp at its sides, appearing at a loss for what to do next. For a moment, only the muted sounds of the storm raging outside disturbed the quiet within the tower.

Then the figure spun and slammed both its fists on the nearest desk. The massive bang it made surprised Erin so much that she let out an involuntary yipping noise. Jarryd remained still as stone beside her. She bit her lip and pressed herself back against the wall, silently praying to the gods that the figure had not heard her outburst. She stood silent, counting the breaths as her heart hammered in her chest. Then a voice called out. It was as harsh as a raven's cry, husky tone full of cold command.

"Who's there?" A sharp, female voice demanded, "Come out before I drag you out!"

Erin and Jarryd locked eyes and he began to pull the blades from their sheaths, but she held out a steadying hand once again. He gave her a disapproving frown, but said nothing as she slowly moved out from the staircase back down onto the landing. As she did, she adopted a slight hunch and clasped her hands before her so hard the knuckles turned white. She clipped her natural gait to a hesitant shuffle, keeping her eyes downcast as she approached the woman. Once she got close, Erin could see that beneath the cloak, the woman was a tall and lean, thin face framed in a dark cascade of locks. She might have been beautiful, had her sharp edged features not been fixed in a sneer that was colder than ice.

"Who are you?" The woman demanded, "And what are you doing lurking around here?"

"I-I'm just an a-apprentice..." Erin raised her pitch and forced a stammer, "I-I didn't mean t-to intrude-"

"I can see you're an apprentice by your robes," the woman cut her off, "what are you doing here?"

"I-I was sent to bring the K-keeper her meal...I-I was j-just coming down when I heard..." She trailed off and swallowed hard.

The dark haired woman snorted, "Of course, I suppose old Aurelia's too good to even eat with the rest of us now."

She paused and eyed Erin, brow raising critically, "Aren't you a bit old to be an apprentice?"

Erin cast her eyes to her feet sheepishly, "I...I'm afraid my talents are...quite limited..."

The dark haired woman nodded, her tone unsympathetic, "Better you recognize it now, and focus on what gifts you do have. I was hoping to avoid seeing that old owl, but I suppose its unavoidable now."

She moved to walk past Erin, but the thief held up a hand to stop her, "P-Pardon, mistress, but the Keeper...she's not in her room."

The woman narrowed her eyes, "What do you mean?"

Erin nodded and motioned down the stairs, "When I got up there, she was gone. I-I left the tray, b-but I don't know when she will return."

The dark haired woman studied her. She leaned in closer, giving Erin a nose full of the strong perfume she wore. It stung her nostrils with the sharp scents of foreign spices and herbs.

"You wouldn't be lying to me, now would you? Aurelia didn't send you down here to get rid of me, did she?"

Erin forced a stricken expression onto her face, redoubling her stammering affect as she shook her head, "N-no! O-of course not, mistress! N-never!"

The woman stared her down for a long moment before seeming to be satisfied with the performance. She snorted again, turning away from Erin and moving towards the stairs. Erin stood frozen in place, continuing to hunch and work her hands nervously in front of her. Before moving down the stairs, the woman turned back and spoke in a low voice.

"If you intend to stay here," she said in a tone like a viper's hiss, "examine your loyalties. Things change slowly in these halls, but when they do, make sure you're on the right side."

With that, she turned and padded down the stairs, light steps echoing in the silence. Erin counted down the moments in long breaths, waiting until she was sure the woman was gone, before she turned and stood up straight. Jarryd came around the corner, still watching the staircase like a hawk.

"That was well done." He gave her an approving nod.

"Just playing a part. What do you suppose she was looking for?" Erin asked in a low voice. She cast a look around the room, examining the chaos the woman had left in her wake.

The Oaren man shook his head, "Whatever it was, she was desperate to find it."

"I don't like this place, Jarryd." She shivered involuntarily as she cast a glance around the room, "There's something off about it. First those people downstairs, now this..."

Jarryd nodded, looking pensive, but remained silent. Erin was going to say more but the sound of footsteps descending the staircase made her lookup. Holton emerged from the passage followed by Barney and Taron. She gave him a hopeful glance but he shook his head. She noticed he had once again pulled the compass out from under his shirt and held it firmly in his hand.

"No luck?'

"No," Holton frowned and worked his jaw, "we'll need to hunt for her."

After taking a moment to gather themselves, they descended the tower and began to follow the compass deeper into the heart of the castle. As they made their way through the labyrinthine halls of the College, it quickly became apparent that something was off. Somehow their path seemed to snake in unnatural and unexpected ways, counter to any inherent sense of direction. A hall that should have led them to the outer wall of the castle somehow opened up onto another intersection, with more paths winding into the gloom. When they stopped at the bottom of yet another staircase for Holton to check the compass, she ran her fingers through her hair and cast a nervous glance around at the others as they waited.

Jarryd's fingers drummed on the pommels of his blades, while Barney constantly popped his knuckles and shot glances from Holton to the empty hallways around them. Even Taron seemed on edge, his casual grin slipping into a frown that made his bearded face look ten years older. She looked out a window and noted how the stairs which should have led them to the main floor left them instead on a level looking down to a courtyard stories below. Her brother chewed at his cheek as he watched the little hands spin for an endless moment before finally coming to settle on one direction. He motioned for them to follow before stuffing the bauble back beneath his shirt, leaving the window as they once again trudged into the dimly lit interior of the school.

It was a long while later when they finally came to something which broke up the monotony of the seemingly endless dark hallways. After descending yet another staircase, they emerged into a large, circular chamber with a vaulted ceiling from which hung a massive, wrought iron chandelier on a great chain. Its metal had been worked into flowing, almost elegant designs and engraved with dreadful figures that were reminiscent of those that adorned the columns and banisters around the school. It dominated the entirety of the circular chamber and loomed over the room's single other defining feature, a massive hole in the ground.

The hole yawned like the maw of some great creature, lined around the perimeter with a winding, downward staircase like a set of unnatural teeth. It was by far the strangest thing they had seen in this strange place. Holton rechecked his compass and showed them all that the hands pointed straight down once again. Erin suppressed the urge to turn and run at the thought of delving into the frozen earth. The others had already begun to gather near the staircase, checking their weapons as they prepared to descend, but she stood where she was. Holton moved to stand beside her.

"Do you want to stay here?" He asked in a low voice, still staring down into the pit, "We could use a lookout."

She shook her head wordlessly, steeling herself against the apprehension that was building like a bonfire inside her. She was distracted. There seemed to be some sort of sound coming from within the hole, like a series of distant, thrumming noises that were muffled and barely audible. Erin tried to strain her ears, leaning forward a bit, hoping to get some sense of what that sound was. A hand on her shoulder brought her attention back to her brother, who stared at her with a worried expression on his face.

"Are you sure you're alright to go down?"

"I'm fine." She insisted, shaking his hand off, "Let's get this over with."

They filed down the spiraling staircase, Holton in the lead and Jarryd in the rear, per usual. The walls were lined with the same dully glowing stones as the rest of the castle, so they did not want for light. But even still, the gloom seemed to grow deeper. The chill wormed its way through their robes, seeping into their very bones. Erin's teeth chattered as she walked and she found herself rubbing her arms to try and coax the warmth back into them. Little rivulets of breath puffed out with every step and snaked up before her eyes before dissipating. The staircase seemed to go down and down, never ending as it spiraled into the darkness.

Eventually, a dark stone floor did materialize below them. It was not carved blocks, as the floor of the castle above them had been, but rather a large sheet of stone, smooth and shining in the low light like river rock. When Holton stepped lightly down, the sound echoed around as though he had stomped with all his might. They all spread out in the circular chamber at the bottom of the pit, trying to peer down the multiple hallways that led off in different directions. There were no markers or indicators to differentiate them, only uneven, arched tunnels through the stone that brought to mind the kind of natural pathways carved by years of underground water flowing through them.

Holton made a noise and called them all back. He motioned for them to follow him down one of the tunnels, along the path the compass indicated. As they moved through the passage, they passed through small pools of witchlight that interspersed the dark every few paces. The thrumming sounds Erin had heard faintly at the top of the pit were louder and more clear now. They were strange, like a pulsing sort of music without beats or breaks. Only several long notes that held as they rose or lowered in pitch. The others heard it now too. Barney cast a curious look at her and Taron cocked his head, trying to make out some sense in the ethereal sounds. But they all kept moving.

Eventually, a faint light appeared out of the darkness ahead of them. It was strange and blue, wavering as though shone through fogged glass. It obscured the end of the passage, even the faint light being so strong in this gloom it made it impossible to see anything in the chamber beyond. They moved towards it like lost miners seeking the sun, pushing through the darkness until they finally emerged into the light.

The tunnel opened up into a wide chamber which stretched in either direction and high up into a barely visible cavernous ceiling from which hung more iron chandeliers on great chains. The strange blueish light emanated from the wall opposite them. Erin had to rub her eyes as she tried to comprehend what they were seeing. An uneven section of what appeared to be some sort of fogged glass was embedded into the stone. It was as tall as the chamber itself and wider than the broadside of two of their wagons. The blue glow was filtering through the glass, a pale, fluctuating light that cast strange shadows across the stone floor.

Looking to either side, Erin could see other sections of glass in the wall a distance away, each with a pool of light spilling through it into the chamber. The sight was so odd and captivating, it took her a moment to notice the figures that stood before the glass wall. Both had been staring towards the wall but had turned to face them when their footsteps announced their entrance. One was an older woman with iron gray hair and a royal blue robe so rich and fine it hardly looked appropriate in the setting. The other was a tall man who wore a dark robe over his obviously lank frame, his white hair and beard familiar.

Chapter Four

Light & Shadow

"What are you all doing down here?" Nolan Felice demanded, all the courtesy gone out of his accusatory tone, "You were told not to wander! I'll see to it that..."

His hands had started to rise but Holton was faster. He had not broken pace and was halfway across the room when his hand came up in a flash. The blade spun across the short distance between the thief and the mage, cold steel catching the wavering light for an instant before it buried itself in the man's pigeon chest. Whatever the thin man had been attempting was interrupted as he screeched in surprise and collapsed. He curled up into a ball, writhing as he whimpered in pain, clawing feebly at the hilt of the blade that now sprouted from his chest.

Beside him the old woman watched without flinching away, not making any attempt to intervene even as Holton approached the fallen man and turned him over with his boot. Her face remained impassive as the thief reached down and ripped the blade out of the fallen mage and at the convulsions the man suffered after. Silently, Jarryd wondered at the person behind that wizened face and gray hair. He watched as she met Holton's gaze evenly, ignoring Nolan as he gasped and shook on the floor a final time before lying still.

"Was all this entirely necessary?" The old woman sighed.

"I had no idea what he would do. Keeper Aurelia, I presume?"

For a moment, she only frowned at him. Then she shrugged and gave a grudging nod, "I suppose you're right. Tell me, who are you, and how is it you found me down here?"

The rest of the crew was spreading out to flank the old woman. Barney and Taron moved to her left while Jarryd moved in a wide arc to her right. They formed a semicircle around Holton and the woman, with Erin guarding the exit. Jarryd rested his hands on the pommels of his swords. Stepping carefully on the slick stone as he eyed the massive glowing wall. Something about it set his nerves on end, but he could not say what.

"I'm just a hired thief, ma'am." Holton's voice was laced with false humility, meeting the woman's iron eyes, "Here to do a job. As for how I found you..."

His hand touched the compass which hung outside his shirt. For the first time, something like surprise flickered across her face. Her eyes widened ever so slightly and her mouth tightened a fraction. Her gaze moved from the bauble to meet the red haired thief's eyes.

"Where did you get that?"

"Oh, I've had it for quite some time now." Holton smirked, "Won it in a game of chance from one of your kind who was down on his luck."

The old woman scowled, "What a waste. Such a piece of craftsmanship falling into the hands of a common criminal."

"Careful now," Holton glanced around at his crew who had now surrounded them, "we were getting along so well."

Aurelia did not deign to cast a glance around at the others, but rather kept her baleful eye fixed on Holton, "Do not threaten me, beast-tongued. You practitioners of the Low Art cannot even begin to conceive of what we do here. Of the skill and knowledge it took to create that artifact you carry around so casually."

Holton blinked and was struck silent for a moment. Jarryd prepared to step forward if called upon, but the thief recovered quickly, like always. Never one to be put on his heels for long, not that one. Jarryd always suspected he would have made a fine soldier in another life.

"Well, either way, you have to admit you're at a disadvantage. And don't think for a moment I'll hesitate to do to you what I did to your compatriot there."

"Violence is ever the refuge of weak minds." She sneered, "Fine, tell me, what is it you have come all this way and gone to all this trouble for?"

"I'm here for Cross' Glass."

"What do you know of Cross' Glass?" Aurelia demanded, moving forward a step, coming within striking distance of Holton. Jarryd adjusted his position as well, moving closer, ever at the ready. Her tone had shifted from uninterested annoyance to one of genuine curiosity as she eyed the thief, "Who are you? What master do you serve?"

"I know nothing of the Glass, only its description and that it is in your possession." Holton answered simply, before giving her a wolfish smile, "And as for masters...I serve no one but myself, ma'am. And what I want, more than anything, is to be on my way back to civilization as soon as possible. So why not just give us the Glass and we'll leave you and your ilk to carry on as you were?"

The old woman stared at Holton for a long moment. She moved her tongue around in her mouth for a bit, seeming to chew on it as she considered. Jarryd struggled to keep his focus on the exchange taking place before him. The hard earned eyes of a master Oaren swordsman strove to be aware of the slightest shift in her stance, the barest twitch of a muscle or flexing of a finger. Anything to indicate that she was moving to strike. But something kept pulling his gaze away.

The light was moving strangely in this chamber, constantly fluctuating as it filtered through the glass wall. Occasionally, the light even seemed to darken for a moment, before returning to normal. It was familiar somehow, in a way he could not put his finger on. The others had seemingly not noticed, all fixated on the confrontation playing out. Jarryd wondered what strange purpose this underground chamber was meant to serve and what was hiding behind these giant panes of fogged glass. It was so alien, so totally unlike any place he had been before. It unsettled him to his very core.

Then there was the noise. A strange chorus of humming sounds that had gotten louder and louder, reaching its crescendo as they entered this room. At first he had struggled to place the odd sounds. But now, closer to the wall, they reminded him clearly of the sounds that had punctuated his childhood as he played on the black beaches of his little fishing village. It sounded like the clarion chorus of whale songs. He forced himself to block the sound out as Aurelia reached one of her weathered hands inside her blue robe. Jarryd tensed, pulling one of his blades out of its sheath a quarter of the way. But he relaxed when she revealed only a glass disk contained in a simple silver ring. It fit easily in her hand, the size of a piece of fruit or a child's toy. She held it up, so that they could all see it plainly.

"If you know nothing of the item you hope to steal, I assume you know nothing of our school, or what we do here?"

Holton said nothing, only returning her steely eyed stare with his own. She waited a moment, then, receiving no response, turned and placed the glass on the wall. It hung there, clinging to the wall as though tacked like a portrait. He waited, tensed to strike, before understanding dawned on him. The sounds that had echoed throughout the cavern had changed. They were no longer simply the ethereal music of whales, but rather, they were more complex. There were notes and breaks, more distinct and detailed than the long, quavering thrumming than before. It sounded almost like words.

"Are they..."

"Speaking, yes. Or what passes for it among their kind." The Keeper interjected, casting a gaze over the great glass wall. The shifting light dimmed as several indistinct shapes seemed to move towards them behind the wall. Jarryd edged closer, standing with his face nearly against the great frosted barrier, seeing the shifting shapes on the other side up close for the first time. They were massive, many limbed things, undulating and flowing in constant motion. Their forms were still blurred behind the glass, but Jarryd thought they might be some sort of beasts with the body similar to a man's but with many long limbs like the tentacles sprouting down from their waists. They brought to mind the nets full of writhing, wriggling squids the fishermen in his boyhood village had brought home in their little boats. The way they moved was entrancing. He had to tear his gaze from their alien forms and force himself to watch the Keeper as the old woman's eyes slid around, taking each of them in with a slow sort of deliberateness. Jarryd saw no fear in that gaze, only a sort of fascination.

"What are they?" Holton asked, his voice low as he stared at the shapes behind the glass. His eyes were narrowed as he listened to what was now clearly identifiable as a spoken language, if not one any of them could understand.

"They are old," Aurelia stated simply, "very old. Creatures from before the time of the Federation, or the Empire. They have been here since there was nothing in the North but ice and trees and wolves."

"Can you understand them?"

The old woman sighed, voice wistful, "Not as well as we would like to. Our founder made the Glass to help communicate with them, but it is an incomplete and imperfect tool. Old Quentin was ambitious, but he lacked the resources of any of the great magical conclaves. If only he had had the support of the University when he built his haven up here."

Holton blinked, then grinned down at her, "So not all you mages are in league, then?"

The slightest hint of a bitter smile played at the corner of Aurelia's own lip, "Oh no. We are as divided as all men are. Cross was a member of the University once, but he disagreed with them vehemently on many issues. He built this place to facilitate those studies that his former colleagues felt were...uncouth."

For a moment, they both fell silent as they eyed the hazy shapes that gathered near the wall. He observed the creatures, it finally dawned on Jarryd what this place was. These chambers of smooth stone had indeed been carved by water. This had once been an undersea cave that had been dammed up by these glass walls. The fluctuating light was filtering into the chamber through the ocean. He wondered at the effort it must have taken to accomplish such a thing. Across the chamber, Barney had taken several steps back from the glass. He and Taron were now trying to watch it and the Keeper simultaneously with wary eyes, unsure where the greatest danger lay.

"Have you learned anything from them?" Holton asked quietly.

"Quite a bit." Aurelia replied, "Many of the secrets of the Old Arts have been lost in the University's quest for control. What little is still known is held hostage in their lofty towers, and they are jealous guardians over their troves of treasures. Creatures like this are the only ties to that bygone age that we have left, hidden away in the far corners of the world."

"Then you won't give me the Glass?"

Aurelia seemed to ponder the question for a bit. Then she asked, "Tell me the person who hired you, and I will consider it."

Holton stared hard at her. Jarryd took a step closer to the Keeper, watching for any signal to strike. The red haired thief sighed, "A man who calls himself the Wizard hired us. We know nothing about him, except that he is in service of a mercenary group called the Burning Blades."

"I thought it might've been that arrogant fool." She shook her head, "He just won't take no for an answer."

She reached up and removed the Glass from the wall. The musical language immediately reverted to the indecipherable thrumming. Now that he had heard it for what it was, Jarryd thought he could discern some of the inflections, even without the aid of the Glass. It seemed to have an agitated edge to it now, rising and falling more quickly, changing pitch in sharper inflections. It might have been his imagination, but he thought the shapes behind the glass were moving more. Their shadowed forms seemed to thrash and writhe. He thought he heard the thud of something beating against the glass among the chorus of sounds. It made the hairs on his neck stand on end and he turned his body slightly to keep a better eye on the creatures behind the wall. Whatever was back there, he did not want to be caught off guard by it.

Aurelia held the Glass up, "What that man wants to do with this...it is dangerous and it will come at a great cost. Has he told you of his plans?"

Holton shook his head. The old woman took a breath, then said, "He is building a machine, one that will change the face of the world. This device will help them extend the power of a mage exponentially, but at a great cost. A great power for one person to wield, to be sure. But it is what they are planning to do with it that is truly..."

The sound of footsteps and voices calling interrupted them, echoing from down the hall. They all turned and saw a group of three gray cloaked mages moving toward them at a quick pace. They had spied the body of the dead mage at Holton's feet and were moving to protect their matriarch. Erin leapt to the ground as one of the mages hurled a great gout of flame down the tunnel which singed the stone and erupted into the chamber with a deafening roar. Almost everyone flinched away from the wave of heat as it washed over them. Barney was the only one who stood his ground, holding out his hands and pulling much of the fire into his grasp like a churning ball.

The Keeper shouted something but it was drowned out as Barney flung the fire back towards the mages who had entered in the wake of the great fireball. Two screeched in panic and dove to either side, trying to avoid the blast, while the third yanked a glowing talisman of some sort from within his robes and held it aloft. The blast of fire encircled him like waves engulfing a small boat, but never touched his body. It only raged around him in a furious storm that battered at his invisible defenses.

Barney was not deterred. He advanced on the man, fire continuing to pour from his hands in rivers of red and orange. The chamber was immediately sweltering with the intensity of the heat. The other two mages were working to regain their footing but Taron had fallen upon one with his knife and they were now wrestling on the ground. Meanwhile, Erin was busy cutting down some sort of vines that had erupted from the third mages sleeves and were trying to ensnare her. Jarryd had moved quickly, taking advantage of the momentary chaos. He drew both his blades and now stood behind the Keeper with one pressed across her neck, and the other across her midsection.

Holton had recovered quickly as well. He stood facing the Keeper, wolfish grin returned to his face, "Stalling for time? I should have guessed."

"You might want to tell your man to stop." Her voice was barely audible over the roaring firestorm that Barney was loosening upon the mage, "Before it's too late."

Holton glanced over. The mage Barney was on the verge of incinerating had gone down to one knee, whatever shield he had erected seemingly losing its strength. Holton gave Aurelia a sly look, "Does that one mean something to you?"

"No." She stated plainly, "But we will all drown if he melts the wall."

For a moment, Holton only stared at her. Then he and Jarryd cast their eyes to the great wall that held back the Coldwater Ocean and whatever monstrosities that were contained within. Little droplets of water had formed all down their surfaces and were racing towards the ground, leaving clear trails across the opaque surface. Not glass then, Jarryd realized with a sinking feeling in the pit of his stomach. These walls were pure ice.

Chapter Five

Ice & Fire

The heat flowed over Barney like the waves off a towering bonfire. It seeped into every muscle and bone and joint in his body, taking him to the edge. As the Fire roared from his hands and cascaded across the mage's defensive shield, he could feel it hunger for more. As he advanced on the kneeling figure, he reached out in every direction and pulled what little heat he could from the air and the stone around him, feeding the greedy hunger of the Fire. He could get at the mage, he knew he could. The Fire knew it could. There was shouting and the sounds of fighting all around him, but he was not going to let this one get away from him. It just needed a little more to break through, and he was going to give it what it needed.

"Barney!"

A pair of hands grabbed his shoulders and shook him so hard his head snapped back and forth. He spun halfway around, one hand still held out towards the kneeling mage, feeding the Fire. Taron was standing there, glaring at him wide eyed with red splattered across his face and beard. He pointed toward the wall.

"Can you not hear, Holt?" He demanded, "Keep it up and you'll bring down that wall!"

Barney glanced over to the leader of their crew, to where he stood before the great glass wall with Jarryd and the old crone. Somehow, it had started shimmering and sparkling while he had been distracted with the mage. It looked like it was covered in thousands of tiny gemstones. It took Barney a moment, but eventually it dawned on him what he was seeing. The little reflective spots were beads of water. The wall was made of ice, and he was melting it. He turned back and closed his fist, only hesitating for a moment. The torrent of Fire died in the space of a breath, leaving the kneeling mage in a ragged circle of scorched and smoking stone.

The mage looked up and blinked, sweat pouring down his face. In an instant he was up and moving towards Barney. The young Northman's legs were wobbly as a newborn foal, and his reaction was sluggish. The mage raised his arm to strike, the air becoming blurred around his fist, but Taron moved too quickly. He swung low with a kick, knocking the man's ankles out from under him. The mage crumpled to the ground, crying out in pain. But it was cut short as the bearded Northman threw a fist into his jaw. The blow sent a spray of red across the stone along with a few white flecks of tooth as the mage crashed face first to the stone and lay still.

All at once, the cold hit Barney as though he had been dunked into the frozen ocean that waited behind the wall. His whole body shook violently, every joint aching as his muscles contracted from the exertion. It was hard to focus. Suddenly, the feeling of sleep reaching up to drag him into the darkness became overwhelming. His vision blurred and doubled. He had drawn on too much power, put too much of himself into the Fire. His knees started to buckle. But then rough hands grasped him by the shoulders and stopped him from collapsing. He forced himself to look up into Taron's grinning face.

"Come on now, boy, ain't no time for all that." The bearded man patted him a little too hard on the cheek, "We got places to be."

Barney managed to swat weakly at the man's hand, grunting as he tried to pull himself together. Taron gave him one last shake and a nod, ensuring he was not going to collapse before turning and stalking off to help Jarryd with the Keeper. Holton had flown across the room to help his sister with the last of the mages, leaving the Oaren holding the Keeper at sword point. As the bearded Northman dragged the old woman's hands behind her back and bound them, Barney raised his eyes, still heavy with weariness, up towards the great wall of ice.

Now that the Fire had subsided, its warmth rapidly having fled from the chamber, the wall had ceased bleeding droplets of water. The icy visage was no longer smooth but was now festooned with thousands of tiny, frozen beads like little blemishes. Behind it, the dark shapes were in constant motion. The wall was still opaque and he could only make out the impressions of whatever it was that loomed out there in the water, but he could see they were agitated. The shapes writhed and squirmed, forms becoming visible as they came and pressed up against the great wall for a moment before darting away again, becoming hazy impressions once more. Barney was gathering his will again, preparing for what was to come, when he noticed something strange.

On the surface of the ice wall, close to where the old woman now knelt on the ground between the two men, something was happening. A small area looked like the surface of a pool of water when you threw a stone into it. Little ripples moved over the surface, barely visible. Barney stared at the spot, unsure what he was seeing or if it was even real. Perhaps it was a trick of the light, or something brought on by the exhaustion and cold that had seeped into him. But then something began to emerge through the spot.

It was the wriggling tip of a gray, fleshy appendage. It shone dully in the low light, like the dead flesh of a fish at the market. The other two did not see it. Jarryd and Taron had become distracted, watching Holton cut down the last of the mages beside his sister. Between them, the Keeper turned in the opposite direction, staring at the wall. Her shoulders were shaking ever so slightly as she watched the great dark shape that lingered there, pressed against the ice. A second tentacle had begun to work its way through the opening before Barney came to his senses.

"*Behind you!*" He croaked at the two men, barely able to force out the words.

Both thieves spun around, Jarryd raising his swords, Taron his knife. But the tentacles moved fast. They shot forth, the first toward the Oaren. Jarryd met it with his blades, slicing upward and drawing a spray of dark blood as he opened a large gash up the side. Taron was not as fast. He swung at the second gray mass but missed and it hit him low, wrapping itself around his leg and yanking him off balance. He cried out as he crashed to the ground with a thud, knife spinning out of his hand.

Immediately, the thing began to drag Taron toward the rippling spot in the wall where two more of the ghastly tentacles had begun to come through. He screamed and Jarryd swung with one sword while still fending off his own tentacle with the other. His blade bit into the thing's flesh but they must have been harder than they looked. He cut a great gash in it, dark blood staining the floor in a long streak, but it remained mostly intact. He raised his sword to swing down again but the other tentacle wrapped itself around his second blade and forced him off balance. He had to use both swords up to fend off the appendage, striking out again and again, to keep it from getting to him. Taron skidded as he was dragged towards the writhing nest of tentacles, crying out for help as he clawed at the stone.

Barney started toward him, forcing his feet to move, but Holton got there first. He leapt at the limb that held the lockbreaker, hacking at it with his hatchet and long knife. Erin was close behind, one of her arms bleeding from some wound she had sustained during her own confrontation. She fell upon the limb as well, stabbing at it again and again. Finally, the thing spasmed and lay still, its grip loosening enough for Taron to free himself. He scrambled away from it, kicking at it with both feet like a child as he shuffled backwards on his hands and backside.

But the reprieve was short lived. Two more of the tentacles had made it through and were moving quickly towards the crew of thieves. Behind those, many more of the twisting limbs were beginning to wriggle through. The spot on the wall reminded Barney of a writhing pit of snakes, a nightmare of withered gray flesh.

Erin and Holton tried to move away from the wall, but they were too slow. One wrapped itself around Erin's wrist, the other around Holton's midsection. They cut and hacked away at the things, but could not keep from being dragged towards the wall where more of the tentacles waited. Jarryd was still cutting away, striking out like a serpent with both his blades, now fending off three of the tentacles. He hacked at the appendages as they came for him, managing to keep them away as he pivoted and danced gracefully back and forth to stay out of their reach. But he could not get closer to help the others. Barney forced himself forward. He shuffled along, until he was near Jarryd.

"We need to get to the others!" The Oaren did not take his eyes from the tentacles as he spoke to him.

They were almost upon the wall now. Other limbs had wrapped themselves around Holton and Erin's legs and arms, pinning them down so they could no longer cut at the limbs. They were crying out for help, struggling in vain as they were drawn inexorably to the nest of writhing tentacles. Barney reached inside and pulled on the last of his reserves. Extending a hand, he felt the Fire flicker to life as he fed it the meager heat left deep inside his body. Even in his sorry state, it felt good. The Fire always felt good when it danced in his hands. It gleamed in his palm for a moment, a bloom of bright red, before it streaked out across the open space between himself and the rippling spot on the wall, moving through the tentacles that Jarryd was keeping at bay. It struck the center of the writhing nest with a massive burst as it spread out in every direction.

The flash was blindingly bright. Jarryd turned his face away, but Barney watched as the Fire flew spread out across all the tentacles, sizzling against the wetness of the gray flesh and sending up a gout of steam. Instantly, the smell of searing flesh filled the air. From the other side of the wall, they heard a great screeching. The whale song had been replaced by a series of jagged, unsettling sounds that made Barney's head feel like it was being clawed at from the inside. As he slammed his hands over his ears, he watched as the gray limbs shook violently. They dropped the Hart siblings and retracted in on themselves, quivering and slamming back and forth, beating against the wall and the stone.

Barney grinned as the wave of exhaustion hit him. His vision blurred even further and he sank down, knees slamming to the stone, the fresh flash of pain barely registering through the fog that had overtaken his mind. Suddenly, there was a sharp cry behind him. He turned his head with an immense effort, and saw Taron standing over the Keeper, the knife in his hand bloodied from where he had dragged it across her neck. The old woman's eyes were wide with shock. She gurgled, blood pouring from the wound and out of the corners of her mouth as it opened and closed wordlessly. Taron put a boot to her back, kicking her to the floor where she twitched for a moment before laying still.

"She was chanting some sorta spell," the bearded Northman said matter-of-factly, "thought it better that she be silent."

Barney turned back to look at the wall, seeing it had solidified once again. The tentacles now flailed about wildly, stuck in place and unable to pull back through. On the other side of the wall, the creature slammed itself against the ice over and over again. The booming sounds echoed throughout the cavern, shaking the very stone. Holton and Erin scrambled to their feet, helping each other regain their footing. Jarryd moved quickly to their side, moving to stand between them and the cluster of writhing tentacles. Barney's head was swimming and he felt himself rocking back and forth on his knees, before something suddenly grabbed him from behind and hauled him to his feet.

Taron had come up beside him and was cursing under his breath as he tried to force the younger man to his feet.

"Come on, you little shit! We gotta get moving before that thing brings that wall down on our heads!"

Barney tried to walk on his own but his legs felt like the bones had gone out of them. He stumbled and tripped and had to put most of his weight on Taron's shoulder as he was carried along. The Northman dragged him until they reached the siblings and all of them stood staring. The wriggling nest of smoldering tentacles were affixed in place, protruding through the ice wall. They still thrashed about as the creature trapped on the other side of the wall fought to free itself. Holton caught each of their eyes in turn, exchanging nods with each of them.

"We need to get out of here, now, before more of those mages show up." Jarryd said as he wiped the dark blood from his blades on his pants legs before sheathing them.

Holton nodded and they all gathered themselves to leave. As Barney was hoisted between Taron and Jarryd, the red haired thief turned back to stride across to the Keeper's corpse. He bent and recovered the Glass from her cold, lifeless hand. Barney watched through bleary eyes as Holton stashed the Glass in his coat, then stopped and stared up at the ice wall for a moment. His back was turned to them as he held up a hand and placed it on the ice. They all watched while he stood there, motionless as stone, as though he were transfixed. Barney, still dazed and barely able to hold onto consciousness himself, thought he heard something new in the strange noises from the other side of the wall.

With the Glass removed, there was no natural separation in the sound, no distinction of one thought from the other. The shrieks and sharp sounds had lost what little resemblance they might have had to human language, once again becoming only a cacophony of ethereal noise. But as Holton laid his hand upon the wall, Barney thought it sounded less alien now. Like maybe knowing that it was a language, having heard its hidden cadences, somehow made him more aware of it. He could not understand it, not truly. But he thought he heard more sharp changes in tone, more notes cut off and replaced with rising harmonies as several creatures spoke as one. He could not be sure, but he thought it sounded angry.

"Holt, let's go!" Erin hissed at her brother. Her voice was harsh and barely contained the dread dripping from every word. Her eyes darted from the wall to her brother and back, "*Please!*"

Holton seemed to come back to himself all at once. He shuddered and turned back to them, pale as a sheet of fresh snow. His face looked thinner somehow and his eyes were distant in a look that Barney recognized. It was the same drained look that probably hung on his own face right now, the look of one when they called upon too much of themselves. The look of someone who had been drained by magic. Holton stumbled a bit as he crossed the space between them.

"You spoke to them?" Barney croaked, voice low and hoarse.

Their leader shook his head, "No, not exactly. It was different somehow, not a conversation. Not like what I do with horses or dogs at all."

"What does that mean?"

"They spoke to me, but not the other way around. It was like their...*voices* were cutting straight through me."

Erin exchanged a worried look with Taron, and Barney shook his head, "I don't understand. But you're alright?"

"I think so." He took a breath and steadied himself, "Yeah, I will be."

"We need to move, boss." Jarryd cut in, "Right now."

Holton nodded and leaned down. He yanked his hatchet out of the mage's back, where he left it during their confrontation. Giving it a quick flick to fling the gore from it, he set his jaw and looked down the tunnel, back towards the stairs that led up to the castle.

"Time to make our exit."

Chapter Six

Rats In A Maze

The group moved as quickly as they could with Barney being mostly carried between Jarryd and Taron, his boots shuffling and skidding across the stone as often as stepping true. As they came hobbling along behind, Holton took the lead, his bloodied knife and hatchet in his hands, and Erin came up right behind him wielding her own blade, still slick with the dark blood of the tentacled beasts. She shivered, as much from the memory of that nightmarish encounter as with the frigid cold down here in this ice cave buried under the earth. Holton paused at the base of the stairs to listen for the telltale sound of footsteps, head cocked to the side like a hound. Had they not been in such a precarious position, Erin might have jabbed her brother with a teasing comment. As it was, she silently hoped his keen ears could keep them from running headlong into another group of angry mages.

When he seemed satisfied, the others readjusted Barney between them and signaled they were ready to continue. They began the slow process of moving up the massive, winding staircase back into the castle proper. It was a heavy task managing the stairs with the weight of a grown man between them. A steady flow of curses poured from under Taron's breath while Jarryd bore the task with his usual steely resolve. As they trudged upwards, the other three began to fall behind. Erin took the opportunity and came up beside her brother, speaking in a low voice, so that only the two of them could hear.

"What was that, back there in the cavern?"

"I have no idea," Holton shook his head, "some sort of ancient sea beasts they've been communing with."

"No, I meant you." She gave him a meaningful look, "Right at the end there, when you went to get the Glass. You said you spoke with them?"

Her brother hesitated for the briefest of moments, a strange look flashing across his face. He glanced back down the tunnel, "No, I...they didn't speak to me, Erin. They spoke into me."

"I don't understand."

"I don't either." He shook his head again. She thought she saw a shiver run through him, which unsettled her more than anything else they had faced thus far, "Animals don't use words to communicate. It's just feelings and images, like hunger or warmth or fear..."

"But this was different?" She prompted when he trailed off.

He nodded, pausing for a moment to let the others catch up, "I felt it inside me...down in my bones. That song, or whatever it is, is powerful. I see why the mages want to understand it."

Erin was not sure if she wanted to know the answer, but she asked the question that was gnawing at her, "What were they saying?"

"They were angry," Holton replied, his voice quiet, "very angry."

Erin stared at him for a long moment, trying to think of a response. But the trio was weaving their way up behind them so she and her brother had to keep moving up the stairs. After what seemed like an age of climbing through the gloom, they emerged back into the large room with the great chandelier hanging over the pit. As Holton and Erin stepped up the last stair they wordlessly moved apart to examine the room, alert for signs of more mages coming to harry them. But the chamber was as empty and quiet as it had been upon their first arrival.

While the others struggled up the last few steps, the siblings made a circle around the edges of the room, checking down the dark halls and meeting again at the main entrance. Erin frowned up at Holton, her brow knitting as she cast a suspicious look into the corridor.

"Where are the rest of them?" She wondered out loud, "Surely if the old girl set out an alarm there would be more than three that responded?"

"The Wizard told us they wouldn't be expecting a heist." His tone conveyed no assurance, "Said they mostly rely on being out here in the ice to keep them safe from thieves and such. Maybe security is just lacking."

Erin gave him a look.

He shrugged, grinning, "Could be we got lucky for once."

"I wouldn't bet on it."

The others came huffing and puffing up the last of the stairs and collapsed in a sweating heap.

"Gods be damned, that's a lot of stairs!" Taron cursed far too loudly. He thumped Barney on the stomach, "You must be getting a gut on you, boy!"

Barney barely managed to shove his hand away. The young man was pale and shaking, lips as purple as if he had been dunked in the Coldwater Sea. Erin moved to his side and began to rub his chest and back in little circles. When she touched his skin it felt as cold and clammy as a dead fish.

"Come on now, Barn. Let's get you warmed back up."

He made an appreciative little noise and laid his head against her shoulder. She kept making the little circles as Jarryd and Taron forced themselves to their feet.

"Get him up," Holton's voice was firm but not unkind, "we can't stay here."

Erin shot him a look, but she whispered encouragement to Barney as she dragged him to his feet. Holton moved over and grabbed the young Northman under one arm, hauling most of his weight onto his shoulder.

"I've got him. Let's go." He pulled the compass out from his shirt, glanced down at the dully gleaming circle and nodded towards the hall.

Erin exchanged a look with Taron, who shrugged and pulled out his knife as he moved to stand beside her. Jarryd took up position as the rearguard, behind Holton and Barney, and they all began to move down the corridor. They trudged along, moving along the path back as well as they could remember it. The dark hallways of the castle all felt similar and it was easy to get one's path confused, but Holton seemed to recall the way well enough. He called out directions at each intersection and fork, hauling Barney along at an admirable pace. Their footfalls echoed in the empty castle, echoing like the approaching march of a squad of attackers. They passed dozens of closed doors and empty chambers, and Erin wondered what the hour was. Could it be that all these people were still in bed? Had they just gotten that lucky?

"These halls are enchanted." Taron whispered under his breath after a while.

She looked over and saw that he had placed his strange eyeglasses on. He was staring around at the stonework slack-jawed, looking like a child struck by his first sight of the sea. She knew they let him see enchantments and spellwork, but she was unsure how far his understanding of their purpose stretched.

"Can you tell what they're meant to do?"

"Hard to tell for certain." He worked his tongue around the inside of his mouth, "Seems to be a kind of mirrored imaging. Make every hallway seem the same, hide distinguishing details, that sort of thing. I'm sure you noticed it already."

She frowned, "To confuse intruders no doubt. They must have some way of getting around it."

"I'd be willing to wager that without that compass we'd be walking in circles until someone came to collect us." His lip twisted in a devilish curl, "It's like a maze, and we're the rats."

"I don't much care for that idea."

"Me neither, do you reckon Holt knows where he's going?" Taron asked her in a low voice after they turned down yet another intersection that appeared identical to the previous several, "Because I have no idea."

She glanced back at her brother, who was trudging gamely along with Barney in tow. A sheen of sweat had broken out across his brow. Jarryd was trailing behind them like a shadow, glancing down each hallway as they passed by.

"Neither do I," she admitted, "but Holt's always had a good sense of direction."

"But you think he can rely on that here?" He cast a meaningful glance around the hallway, "The compass got us to the old woman, but it doesn't have anyone outside to find that I know of."

Erin frowned and cast another look over her shoulder. She bit her cheek for a moment before making her decision. She stopped walking and turned to face her brother.

"Are we lost, Holton?"

The others all stopped short and looked from one redheaded sibling to the other. Barney started to speak, but Erin silenced the young Northman with a look. Holton took a moment to gather himself, readjusting weight he had slung across his shoulders. Finally, he reached into his shirt and pulled out the compass. It glimmered in his palm as he held it up so they could see. All the hands pointed forward, along their path.

"The old woman's dead. Who's it tracking now?" Erin demanded, crossing her arms.

"One of the oxen." Holton grinned, "Pocketed a few of its hairs on the way in here."

"You're a mad bastard, Holt." Taron's grin was so wide it threatened to split his face apart, "Never would have thought of that myself."

Erin was about to say something when the sound of voices came echoing along the halls from somewhere behind them. Wordlessly, they all turned and kept moving down the hallway as quickly as they could. They followed Holton's direction until they emerged into a long corridor with statues of beasts on one side, facing a row of tall windows on the other. As they moved down the hall, Erin looked out one of the tall windows to see if she could determine how much time had passed during their foray into the subterranean lair.

The moon still hung high in the sky, its glowing visage staring down at them through the haze of icy wind and swirling snow. She could not see much beyond the immediate area outside the windows, just a few feet of snow covered courtyard before anything beyond was lost in the darkness and storm. There was nothing to indicate where in the castle they were, no landmark against which to map their progress. The voices came again, seeming closer than before. The telltale harsh tones and shouts of anger clearly indicated that their misdeeds had been discovered.

"Shit." She heard Holton curse.

She turned to see what had upset him and saw him staring down at the compass. All the hands pointed towards the windows. He met her eyes and grimaced.

"It only shows the direction. Doesn't care nothing about walls and such."

"Should we just force our way out?" She asked, not relishing the idea of continuing their seemingly endless trek through the castle.

"It'd take some doing," Taron was examining the glass through his spectacles, "they're warded up tight."

"But you can get through it?"

The bearded man nodded and clicked his tongue, "Sure enough, given some time."

She turned to look at Holton, who was easing Barney down to the floor. He nodded, "Do it. This castle is too tricksy for my liking. The sooner we're out of here the better."

Taron grinned and pulled out his roll of tools, laying them out gingerly on the floor before him. They took up positions around the lockbreaker, eyeing either entrance to the hallway as he went to work with his delicate instruments. It was not long before the first mage came barreling through the entrance at nearly a full sprint, cloak billowing out behind him. He had the look of an apprentice, smooth faced and young, seemingly more than a little surprised to have actually found the intruders.

"They're here-*argh!*" He was cut off as Holton closed the gap between them with astounding speed, his hand closing around the young man's neck in one swift motion. The mage gargled and brought up his hand, now glowing with a pale blueish green light, but Holton caught him by the wrist and slammed the boy's head bodily into the nearest of the monstrous statues. He slumped to the ground like a dropped sack of wheat flower and did not move. He stared down at the boy for a moment, grimace carved into his features.

"How much more time do you need?" Holton demanded as he looked up to scan the hallway for more approaching attackers.

"Just a bit longer..." Taron grumbled through his teeth. He was holding some sort of copper rod between them as he worked, brow furrowed in concentration. Erin thought this must be a more difficult enchantment than he was used to dealing with.

Just then, they heard a shout cut off by a sickening squelch. Jarryd had cut the throat of another apprentice who had been unfortunate enough to enter through the side he was guarding. The young woman gargled and clawed at her throat, panic making her eyes go wide as she thrashed about, speckling the dark stone with red spots. By the time she collapsed into a heap on the floor, the sounds of more footsteps and shouting had grown closer.

A crashing sound brought all their heads snapping back to Taron. A series of metal disks hung all around the edges of the window frame he had busted open with his elbow. A blast of frigid air slammed into the hallway, hitting them all like a punch in the gut. Erin felt the sting of cold on her face as she saw Taron wipe away the shards of glass with his elbow and wave them on.

"Come on, you lot," he put his hands on the windowsill and heaved himself up, "I'll go through first and you all pass me the ki-"

Taron was cut off by a deafening snap like bones breaking as he moved into the open pane. His body went unnaturally rigid. Frozen, he fell backward and crashed to the floor with a thud. Then he began twitching and shaking in spasming bursts where he lay on the stone. His eyes were blinking, out of sync with each other, and his teeth were clenched so hard the veins in his neck stood out like small ropes, visible even beneath his beard. Erin ran to him, dropping to her knees beside his shaking body. She could feel his muscles convulsing with dozens of tremors beneath his clothes.

"What happened?!" Barney cried out hoarsely. He had crawled across the floor to where Taron lay, on the side opposite to Erin. The young man had regained enough of his color to pale visibly when Taron hit the floor. He screamed the bearded Northman's name as he leaned over and shook him.

Holton swore as he crossed the room to his fallen friend. He pulled Barney off the fallen lockbreaker and looked him over quickly. The tremors seemed to grow less severe after a few moments, but Taron either could not hear or could not respond when they called out his name. Holton cursed again and looked around. Erin met his eyes, doing her best not to panic.

"He must've missed something." She said in a low voice, "We don't have time to let him recover. We have to keep moving."

Holton gritted his teeth before nodding, "I'll get Taron, you help Barney. Jarryd will take point."

He looked past her to where the Oaren swordsman stood, face stony as he stared down at them. As her brother stood up, hauling up the still spasming form of the bearded Northman, Erin moved to help Barney. The young man had regained some of his strength, not needing the same support he had to make it up the stairs. She could feel the heat had returned to his body and he waved her off as she attempted to place his arm over her shoulders.

"I'll be alright." Barney told her with a weak grin. He wobbled a bit on his feet but managed to keep from falling.

She nodded and they both looked to Holton. He grimaced as he hefted Taron's body up across his shoulders like a pack. He winced but made no complaint, only giving them a curt nod. They all turned and moved to the other end of the hall, past the corpse of the woman Jarryd had killed only a few moments earlier, and delved back into the black halls of the castle.

Chapter Seven

Shadow & Silence

As he led the way through the halls, the sounds of his companions struggling along behind, Jarryd wondered what other witchcraft and treachery waited for them in these halls. He had thought Holton rash for taking this job in the first place, but the thief had never steered them wrong before. The man had an uncanny knack for knowing what jobs to take and which ones to walk away from, and for keeping all their necks from the noose. But this went beyond anything they had attempted before. He knew the payout would be monumental, but did it matter if they were not around to collect?

Jarryd pushed the thoughts from his mind with a practiced effort, breathing in long, low breaths and refocusing on the task at hand. He could not afford distractions now, he had to stay sharp. With two of their number incapacitated and the entire castle likely on their trail, it would take everything they had to make it out of here with their hides intact. He scanned their path as Holton called out directions, seeking anything that appeared odd or out of place, any sign of the enemy he knew was bearing down on them, getting closer by the moment.

He turned aside at the last second. Just as what had appeared to be another decorative suit of armor in the intersection of two hallways swung its halberd down towards his head, he pivoted his body aside. It slashed through the air less than a hands-width from his face. It had been the stance that gave it away. The way its weight sat forward on its toes rather than back on its heels as all the others had. It had been anticipating the swing. The suit of armor's halberd came crashing to the floor, sending sparks and bits of stone flying and leaving it off balance. As he stumbled backwards Jarryd's hand flew to his side, drawing one of his blades and striking in a single, fluid motion. Using his momentum, he spun on his heel and brought the sword around in a wide arc, catching the side of the helmet as it tried to recover from the missed swing.

Instead of the sound of metal clanging on metal, there was the unmistakable wet thud of steel slicing through flesh. As the thing stumbled and fell, its illusion fell away like fog drifting off a lake. All that was left was a young man with a shock of black hair and eyes as wide as Southlander dinner plates above the streak of red that ran across his face. Jarryd's blow had cleaved a gash across his youthful visage and he lay screeching and clawing at the wound until the Oaren drove his blade through his heart. The blow was a mercy, ending the apprentice's suffering in the space of a breath.

The others stared at the young man's corpse as Jarryd freed his blade from his chest and wiped the gore off on his cloak. Holton recovered the quickest, meeting Jarryd's eyes and giving him a nod of approval. His face was covered in sweat from hauling Taron this far. The Oaren nodded back and turned to continue on their path when the sounds of shouting came from behind them, entirely too close for comfort. He looked to the others and motioned down the hallway.

"You all go, I will hold them off."

Erin shook her head, but Holton met Jarryd's gaze with ice in his eyes, "You're certain?"

Jarryd nodded again, "Get them out of here. I'll catch up."

Erin and Barney both started to protest, but Holton silenced them with a look, "We have to get Taron out of here. Jarryd can handle himself."

Despite the others looking like they wanted to argue, they held their tongues. As they marched past him, Holton paused for a moment and met Jarryd's eye. The red haired thief grinned wolfishly.

"Don't die, brother. You still owe me."

"Dying in debt would be a great dishonor."

He nodded to Holton, before the other man readjusted the weight of the unconscious man he carried. Taron's head lolled back and forth with each step and he moaned wordlessly, but he seemed to have finally stopped twitching. Jarryd said a silent prayer beneath his breath for the talented lockbreaker. He hoped whatever trap had been tripped would leave no lasting mark. Erin started to speak as she and Barney followed her brother, but Jarryd shook his head and motioned them down the hallway. She gritted her teeth but forced herself to continue with visible effort. He watched them shuffle down the corridor for a moment, but the sounds of rapidly approaching footsteps brought his attention back to the task at hand.

As the others fled down the hallway, Jarryd drew his second blade and breathed the chill, dry air in deep, taking a moment to collect himself. The cold burned as it filled his nostrils. No matter how long he had lived in the North, the air never quite agreed with him. But here, at the far edge of the world, it prickled inside his throat and chest. The sound of shouting and stomping feet was close now, and he knew they would be on him in a matter of moments. He blew out a long, low breath and stepped off the main hallway. He pressed his back against the wall and let the shadows swallow him up. He held his twin blades low at his sides, poised to strike.

A few breaths later the first of the mages came around the corner, a hefty man with a great bushy beard that did little to conceal his ruddy cheeks. He barreled down the corridor towards the form of the slain mage, audibly huffing and cursing under his breath as he did, moving right past Jarryd's hiding place. Behind him came three more mages, a woman with red hair and then two men. All but the fat mage looked young, likely more apprentices. The swordsman remained unnoticed as they hurried to crowd around the body and argue over what to do next. Untrained, undisciplined academics, unprepared for this sort of conflict. Jarryd felt his mouth curve in the barest hint of a smile as he waited for the right moment.

After some arguing and wild gesticulating, the bearded man shouted down the others and commanded them all to follow him in pursuit of the intruders. He began to hustle down the hall and the woman followed shortly behind. The two men hesitated only a moment, but it was long enough. Jarryd sprung from the shadows, crossing the space between them in a few rapid strides. He sliced downward with one sword, bringing his blade across the first man's back. As the red streak sprayed blood out across the stone floor, the man's scream filled the hall. Jarryd used the momentum of his swing to spin and meet the last of the mages head on.

This pursuer was a young Northerner, his face unlined and blonde hair so fine it was like a cloud of thistledown. He was far too young for this. But even still, Jarryd did not hesitate. To hesitate meant death on the battlefield, a lesson this one would never learn. As the young mage tried to raise his hands in defense, the Oaren warrior thrust his second blade into his chest. The thud of impact sent a tremor down his arm. Jarryd watched the young man's robes bulge for a moment before they tore to reveal the short blade as it emerged out of his back. The young mage gasped in surprise, unable to cry out as all the air leaked from his lungs.

Without ceremony or flourish, Jarryd pulled the blade from his chest and let him collapse to the floor. Behind him the first of his victims was wailing as his blood puddled on the floor, screaming and crying out for his companions to turn back. Jarryd smoothly stepped across the hall and moved down an opposite corridor from the one he had been hiding in. He could hear the shouts as the hefty mage and the woman turned back, screaming in surprise as they saw what had happened. Jarryd did not turn to check if the other mages had stopped to help their fallen friend, but stalked down the hallway at a quick pace until he found another bend. Turning left around the corner, he worked his way down the hall until he found another left turn. Behind him there was a rush of air that roared down the hallway he had just exited. He could hear the powerful blast knock down portraits and send various other decorations crashing to the floor. Even down this side hallway, it clawed at his coat and whipped around him, threatening to force him off his balance.

He tried doors as he passed them, finding them all locked against the night. He had neither the skill nor the time for lockbreaking as his fallen comrade had, and so he delved further into the castle, always trying to make left turns when possible in an attempt to circle back around. Eventually, he found himself in a wide hall with a raised ceiling. It was the dining hall they had attended earlier, with long tables and benches which ran down the center. He moved around the perimeter, stepping lightly, blades still held at the ready as his sides. There were too many entrances to this room, too many angles to keep up with. He thought it was likely a poor place to linger. As he hurried across the room towards the next entrance, a figure emerged from the hallway.

It was the fat mage, his great gut swinging back and forth under his bushy beard as he strode into the room. He glared at Jarryd, his watery eyes narrowed over his flushed cheeks. Jarryd waited for him to say something, but the mage simply lifted his hands, pudgy fingers splayed out wide to either side of him. Inky darkness spread out from his fingertips like a fog, blotting out every sliver of light as it engulfed the space around him. Jarryd lifted both his blades to the ready as the cloud of darkness flowed out across the walls and ceiling, swallowing up the dining hall so rapidly he barely had time to register what was happening. He finally realized the perilous position he was in and began to dash the final few paces towards the mage, trying to close the distance before he lost the last of the light.

But the darkness closed in around him before he could reach the mage, enveloping the last hint of light and leaving him staring at nothing in every direction. As he slowed to a stop, he realized he could no longer hear his own footfalls on the stone. The wailing of the storm as it beat against the windows and castle walls was now only the barest of whispers. All around him was seemingly empty, only endless black and silence. He stopped and stood still, barely breathing as he strained his ears for the slightest noise. He fought the hammering in his chest, forcing himself to stay calm. The moments dragged on and on, the quiet growing deeper with each passing breath. His skin prickled in the cold, one thing that had not been deadened by this veil of shadow. How unfortunate, he thought to himself, he would have welcomed a reprieve from this damnable chill. But he again pushed the thought from his mind and focused.

The sensation was so subtle he almost missed it. The barest huff of hot air being breathed out, accompanied by the unpleasant scent of sweat and body odor. He moved all at once, ducking to the side and swiping his blade out in a wide, horizontal arc, right at waist height. He could not see what his blade struck, could not even make out the hilts in his own hands the darkness was so total, but he was rewarded with a gasp of pain and the muffled sound of liquid hitting stone. He struck out with his second blade, stabbing at where he had made contact in a lunge. The thud of metal hitting flesh and the sound of a gasped breath told him he had hit his mark.

The darkness began to fade, turning from total black to a dark gray, then a light haze. Jarryd saw the cross guard of his blade materialize out of the gloom, followed by the ichor covered blade emerging from the chest of the fat mage above the long slice across his belly. He still held a shaky hand outstretched, jagged knife in hand, poised to strike as though he had not yet registered what had happened to him. His watery little eyes were as glossy as gemstones now. Jarryd freed his blade in one motion and the mage collapsed in a heap on the ground, knife skidding away over the stone, taking the last of the magical darkness with him.

The crackling sound alerted him a moment too late. He started to turn, to raise his blades defensively, but the blazing ball of white light moved across the room like a streak of lightning. It missed its mark, a glancing blow by the grace of God, but still the heat of the blast seared his clothes and skin with its intensity. He gritted his teeth as the smell of charred flesh filled his nostrils, stumbling across the open space away from the body of the dead mage even as a second blast followed the first. He heard the eruption roar and reverberate in the wide room as the first ball of light hit the wall behind him, dropping both his blades and throwing himself down to his belly to get out of the way of the second. It missed him by a finger's length.

The blast streaked through the air where he had been a fraction of a moment before. The crackling energy made the hairs on his neck and arms stand up and he silently swore as he forced himself to ignore the pain, roll over his burned side, and clamber to his knees to face his assailant. The red haired mage was advancing on him, another ball of light at the ready in her raised hand. She hefted it like a stone, throwing it at him with a fierceness in her eyes flashing from under her mess of auburn curls. He dove behind one of the long tables as the ball struck the stone where he had just been and erupted into a blinding shower of sparks that rained down on him in stinging rivulets.

Jarryd wasted no time. From his crouched position, he placed both his hands on the edge of the table and pushed as hard as he could, raising it up on its edge. It was made of heavy timber wood and he had to strain his muscles so hard he thought he felt something tear, but he managed to bring it on its end. Hunched behind it, he waited and listened. He heard the woman's soft footsteps on the stone, getting closer and closer. He knew she was prepared to send another of the explosive blasts as soon as she caught sight of him. He reached into his pocket and pulled out a small sack of coins. All he had left from their job in Greyhaven. He bounced the pouch in his palm a few times before he lobbed it to his left, then, without waiting, dashed around the right corner.

The woman had been caught off guard by the deception, her attention turned away momentarily, but she had not launched her ball of magic fire at it as he had hoped. She spun back to face him, blazing ball of white light in her raised palm ready to strike. He flew across the short distance between them, pumping his legs hard and throwing himself into a diving run as she brought the ball down towards him. Jarryd threw his arm up just in time to stop the motion, catching her by the wrist, using the momentum to yank her off balance. She yelped as she was spun against her will, falling backwards into him. The maneuver had left him holding her wrists in front of her, with the ball of light still cradled in her upward palm.

Jarryd gave her no time to stop what was coming. He turned her palm inward and forced it towards her body. She screamed and tried to pull away, but the white fire had already spread to her skin. He released her writhing body as it roared and erupted across her chest, shoving her away as it engulfed her in the blink of an eye. She wailed ear splitting screeches that echoed around the chamber until her throat burned away and all that was left of her was a charred and smoldering corpse. Jarryd stared at her for a moment after she was gone. His eyes had to adjust to the retreating of the blaze and the return of the low gloom that was the castle's normal interior.

Finally, he pushed himself to his feet, feeling his burnt side like a thousand hot needles where the woman's blast had grazed him, and stumbled to collect his two blades. He wiped off the blood and remnants on the fat mage's robes before stowing them back in their sheaths, meticulous in their care despite the dire situation. Then he turned and moved toward the hall the dead man had entered through, delving back into the seemingly endless halls once again.

Chapter Eight

Fire On The Ice

Barney had mostly regained his composure by the time they reached the main corridor. His hands still felt shaky and there was a chill that hung heavy in his chest, but he could walk without assistance and even help Holton with his load a bit. Taron, by contrast, still as boneless as a sack of grain, now being dragged along between them. Holton was red faced and sweating, his eyes locked straight ahead as his chest heaved visibly under his robes. When they emerged from yet another corridor into the grand main hallway with the ornately carved pillars and grand double staircase, they all breathed a sigh of relief, but none more so than their leader. He took on the burden of Taron's weight by himself once again and told Erin and Barney to go ahead to make sure the way was clear.

The two moved down the hall at a deliberate pace, nearly in step with each other. The hall was deathly quiet, the only noise coming from the muffled sound of the wind howling outside. At about the halfway point, something caught Barney's eye. There was a figure standing near the entrance doors. It was wearing a black robe, and in the low light it blended in neatly with the stone. The figure's shadowed face was turned towards them and seemed to be watching their approach. Barney held out a hand to catch Erin and motioned towards the figure. She stopped short and her eyes went wide.

Holton exchanged glances with the other two. He gently lowered the limp form of the lockbreaker to the floor and took a breath before stepping forward between them. He paused, speaking low enough for only the two of them to hear.

"If they make a move, take Erin and run." Holton whispered under his breath.

Barney gave him a nod and watched as he moved forward to face the mage. The cloaked figure stepped forward, the light pushing back the shadow cast by his cowl enough to reveal her face. Underneath, it was all hard angles and piercing eyes beneath a shock of dark hair. She looked Holton up and down with an appraising eye, her mouth turning up at the corner in a crooked grin that seemed to reveal entirely too many teeth. It reminded Barney of a snowcat's maw. Erin came up beside her brother, voice frayed and tinged with suspicion.

"What are you doing here?" She asked, tone equal parts suspicion and bewilderment.

Barney struggled to catch up, but saw that Holton regarded his sister with the same confusion. The woman turned to face her, amusement glinting in her eyes.

"I could ask you the same thing. I thought you were an apprentice sent to fetch the Keeper's supper?"

Erin stared back at the woman in silence, defiant as she met her icy gaze. Barney reached out to the Fire and tried to stoke the smoldering heat within him. But it was still dampened by his earlier exploits, and the area around him was devoid of much heat. He could add little to his already meager reserves.

"Are you here to stop us?" Holton asked the woman. He stood at a slight angle to her, hand on hilt of his knife. Barney had seen what he could do with that blade, even at a distance, but he was unsure what game this newcomer was playing.

"If I was, you think you would all still be standing here?" The shadows played across her face strangely as she answered. Her tone the kind that filled Barney with a desire to burn things.

To his credit, Holton did not take the bait. He stared her down and waited for what came next. Her smile faltered a bit as her intended jibe failed to elicit the response she had obviously been hoping for. She shifted her foot from one foot to the other.

"The old woman is dead then?"

Holton narrowed his eyes, "Aurelia?"

"Of course."

He nodded and her feline grin widened once again, "Finally. I thought that crotchety old owl would never release her talons."

"Who are you? And what do you have to do with this?"

She gave him another smile, "Why, I am the next Keeper of Coldwater."

Holton considered this pronouncement for a moment, "You're working with the Wizard?"

She did not respond, but rather waved her hand in a dismissive motion, "You better get moving if you're going to get out of here. Most of the others are still looking through the halls, but my little distractions will only keep them from your trails for so long."

Holton looked as though he wanted to wring the answers from her slender form, but he only glared at her before turning toward Barney and his sister, "Bring Taron, we need to move."

"Not that way," the mage said as Holton took a step toward the large main doors, "there's a conclave of mages out in the courtyard waiting on the off chance you made it out."

She waved a hand and a small side door flung open off to the side, "That way will take you out to the East Yard where the stables are."

They all stared at her for a moment before gathering up the now groaning Taron and moving towards the open doorway. Erin led the way as they moved into the hallway and out of the central chamber. Holton was grumbling something under his breath about the mischief of mages as he shouldered Taron's weight, so as Barney brought up the rear, he was the only one to see the woman step backwards into the shadow and vanish as though she had never been there at all.

When they finally emerged from the castle into the storm, they were immediately assaulted by the torrent of wind that howled through the blackened tundra. It buffeted them back and forth and clawed at their exposed faces with frigid fingers like an animal bent on dragging them down. They fought the entire way across the open yard, trudging through the knee deep snow and slipping on slick cobblestone. The outer wall of the castle slowly took shape through the wind driven snow, a hulking mass that stretched out into nothingness either direction.

Positioned against the wall's base, a long, low building waited for them. It was difficult to see, squatting in the shadow of the outer wall and entirely dark, but they found their way to it eventually. The massive outer doors were bolted shut, but it was a mundane lock which was quickly smashed off with the blunt end of Holton's hatchet. As they stumbled inside they all breathed a sigh of relief to be out of the storm and once again inside.

As they entered, the dormant witchlights embedded in the ceiling came to life, emitting a pale glow throughout the building. The stable was one wide, low ceilinged structure that stretched out seemingly endlessly in either direction. In addition to the witchlights, stones which pulsed with an orange glow hung from the ceiling in metal baskets. They were interspersed at regular intervals and gave off waves of pleasant heat, warming the dozens of animals that were being sheltered here from the foul weather. Barney and Holton looked at each other before dividing and moving in opposite directions, leaving Erin to mind the still recovering Taron near the entrance. Barney picked his way down the aisle, past pens of unshorn sheep and hair-covered cows as he hunted their wagons.

After what seemed like an eternity, he found a break in the stalls where vehicles were kept. It was a large, open space with its own set of entrance doors, filled to the brim with a medley of carts and wagons and one ornately decorated carriage all jumbled together to try and fit them all. Had he been after one of the others, it might have taken a great deal of effort to disentangle it from the rest. But luckily, the three wagons that made up their train had been set to the side and kept easily accessible. He spied their oxen team in a pen on the opposite side of the sea of vehicles, and decided luck was on their side this month. He dug out a smooth, black stone from his pocket and spoke into it, nearly placing his lips on the runic designs that inscribed its surface. It shone brightly for a moment, then was once again only a pretty stone. He stowed it and turned back to retrieve the others.

Holton arrived almost simultaneously back at the entrance, having heard the call through. They all helped haul Taron down the aisle and laid him in the back of the lead vehicle. As Holton and Erin worked on getting the oxen out of the pen and all harnessed, Barney moved to the rear wagons. They appeared empty, but as he ran his hands under the notch on the side panels of the second wagon he found the hidden latch. The side dropped down, revealing two heavy crossbows, each with their own quiver of large bolts.

These were not the common kind meant for hunting, like those they had turned over upon their arrival. They were wicked looking weapons with gear driven, repeating mechanisms, with pulls strong enough to pierce armor. He threw the crossbows and quivers over his shoulders, then reached over to the other side, repeating the process but this time revealing two burlap sacks behind the hidden compartment. With a grunt of effort, he hauled them up and moved back to the first wagon. Taron was groaning as Barney dropped the sacks beside him, and the young Northman took a moment to kneel down and pat him awkwardly on the shoulder.

"Try not to die, old man." Barney told him before standing and stepping out onto the driver's seat.

Erin and Holton had the first wagon hooked up with four of their oxen and were running a last check to ensure the straps and buckles were all fastened. As he stepped out, Holton looked up at him.

"Are you ready for this? If you can't do your thing, this isn't going to work."

"I'll be fine." He grinned as he tossed Holton one of the crossbows and Erin the other, "You just make sure to do your part."

Holton nodded, "We need to make sure-"

But the metallic screech of a lock being splintered apart cut him off as the doors came slamming open. Accompanied by a brutal blast of frigid wind, a contingent of mages stormed into the barn, their robes snapping and swirling around them so they appeared like dreadful wraiths descending on the company of thieves. They wasted no time with questions. The first threw a shower of pale green sparks from his fist towards Erin, who barely managed to fall backwards, just out of his range. The sparks showered the floor and sizzled on the stone, leaving an array of little pockmarks that smoked with rivulets of white smoke.

As she fell, Erin hefted her crossbow and pulled the trigger. A bolt flew up into the mage's chest with a meaty thud. He gasped in surprise as the wind was knocked out of him. He twisted unnaturally in mid-step, his second fistful of deadly green light opening as he fell and spilling down over his own lower body. The searing sound of first cloth, then the flesh of his legs, could be heard even over the commotion of the fighting that had erupted in the wake of their entrance.

The second and third cloaked figures stopped just inside the entrance, more reserved than their over enthusiastic and unfortunate partner. The first, a small man with a pencil mustache and a rat face flung a handful of thin, guard-less blades into the air. They arced up in a lazy spin and then all froze in place and pointed down, towards Holton. He realized what was happening just as they dove downwards at him like a flock of angry hawks. Barney called out but was cut off by the blast of force that knocked him off his feet and sent him tumbling back through the canvas flap that separated the wagon's bed from the driver's seat.

He fell into the wagon, slamming to the floor beside Taron, and all the air was knocked out of him. It felt like an invisible ram had slammed its horned head into his chest and he was unsure if it had been caved in for a terrifying moment. He fought to pull breath back into his chest, barely able to manage the smallest of gasps. He struggled up to his knees through a coughing fit and forced himself to crawl back through the canvas flap, his eyes were watering and unfocused. In the low light of the stable and the stinging frozen wind, he had to shake his head a few times to clear the haze and properly make out the conflict that was happening around the cart.

Holton seemed to be dueling an invisible foe as he fended off two of the blades that floated around him at once. He struck out with both his weapons constantly, slashing one of the blades out of the air with either his long knife or his hatchet only for it to rise again almost immediately. With dismay, Barney saw that alongside a number of fresh wounds which streaked his hands and arms with bright scarlet, that Holton had the third blade lodged high in his right shoulder, its hilt gleaming in the amber light. Opposite him, Erin was trying to fend off the third mage, the one who had caught him by surprise.

She sent bolt after bolt flying at him, but he was batting them out of the air with concussive blasts of force seemingly summoned with dismissive waves of his hand. Each one sent little waves of hay and dust scattering across the barn away from him. Erin was forced to retreat behind a column to keep from getting knocked over, waiting for each of the mage's blasts to subside before ducking out to fire another volley. Barney reached inside and to grasp the Fire again. It was easier here, out of the snow and in the warmth of the stables. He felt it smoldering there, ready and anticipating, somewhat recovered from its near extinguishing before. It sparked to life in his palm, a red bloom that grew until it was a ball of spitting fire. The rat faced mage still stood near the entrance, moving his hands like a puppeteer, manipulating the blades from a safe distance.

Barney hurled the ball of fire into the mage's chest. He grinned as it burst with a roar and a blinding flash of light, the flames spread across his robes. The rat-faced man screeched and flailed wildly until Holton's hatchet streaked across the open space between them and embedded itself in his guts. He dropped to the floor in a motionless heap as the fire consumed him. Holton wasted no time, ripping the blade from his shoulder and sending it sailing across the space between him and the mage that was harrying his sister. The mage knocked it aside with the same casual flick of the wrist, but as he did Erin took the moment and loosed another bolt towards him.

The mage tried to bring his hand up to summon another blast of force, but the bolt was too fast, catching him in the shoulder. He screeched in pain, falling to his knees and clutching at the shaft. Erin closed the distance in the flash of an eye. He looked up and came face-to-face with the crossbow as she leveled it against his face. He opened his mouth to say something, perhaps to plead for his life, but she pulled the trigger before he had time to speak. The gears clicked, releasing the bowstring with a resounding twang, and the mage's corpse fell to the ground and stained the straw red from the wound in his face.

Around them the stable had descended into chaos. The animals were crying out, snorting and hollering, filling the space with a cacophony of discordant sound that overwhelmed even the howling of the wind through the open doorway. They were bashing themselves against their cages and kicking and biting at each other as they panicked and tried to get free. Several had managed to break loose from their confines and were charging wildly around the aisles, searching for a way to get out into the open air.

Their own oxen were snorting and tossing their heads against their reins, dancing back and forth and trying to free themselves from their leads. It seemed pure luck that they had not already run and dragged the wagon with them. Holton hissed and cursed as Erin and Barney helped him climb up into the wagon, gripping at his wounded shoulder. He took the driver spot and handed the crossbow off to Barney.

"I'll be no good with it, like as not." He grumbled, wrapping the reins around his hands, "But I can keep these beasties on track.

Barney noticed the red haired thief's eyes go a little distant, and the oxen calmed a bit. They ceased trying to throw their reins and settled into disconcerted grunting. That was when they heard the shouting. Outside, the day had finally started to break in the distance. Pale red and orange were erupting in the western sky through the haze of storm winds and cloud cover. It barely drove the darkness back at all, but the light was just strong enough for Barney to see a whole host of robed figures rushing through the swirling snow towards them.

Chapter Nine

Fight To The Fjord

Taron's head was throbbing so hard it felt like it was being ripped apart. He felt as though he might be sick and, even through the fog in his brain, he knew he did not want to do it all over himself. He tried to push up to his elbows, but was immediately sent back down as the floor lurched under him. As his head bounced off the wood he cursed, trying not to pass out again.

"Stay low!" He heard Holton yell from somewhere near his feet.

He pushed himself up to one arm and stared down towards the front of the wagon. From his vantage point, most of his vision was taken up by the backs of his three comrades. But beyond that, he could make out the form of a large, ruined doorway just before they hurdled through it out into the freezing open air. He scrambled to his hands and knees and tried to crawl forward, doing his best as the cart rumbled and jostled him back and forth. He heard the cracking of reins and the sound of Holton spurning the oxen forward as he stuck his head up through the flap just in time to watch as the thief drove the wagon through the middle of a smattering of robbed shapes.

Various blasts of colored light went careening off in random directions as the mages were forced to leap out the way. Erin and Barney were manning the crossbows, sending a volley of bolts after the robed shapes as they tumbled away in the snow. They worked the action on the crossbows quickly, working the levers after each shot and immediately loading another bolt in the track with uncanny speed. It seemed all the training they had done with these new weapons had paid off. The wagon jolted around wildly, picking up speed incredibly fast with the four oxen now only loaded down with a single wagon and four passengers.

"Barney, the bags! Use one to get them off our tails!"

Barney nodded and spun around, coming face to face with Taron for the first time. A wide grin cracked his face.

"You're awake!"

"Barely." Taron grumbled, "Feels like I was run over by this wagon."

The young man clapped him on the shoulder and leapt into the back of the wagon without comment. He saw there were two of the large sacks he had packed away into the secret compartments of the wagons. Barney lifted one with both hands and walked it to the rear door. He kicked the door open, almost falling over himself in the process. Out the back, Taron could see the shapes of the mages moving after them. They seemed to be gliding along the snow far too quickly for normal men. They were, in fact, catching up to the fast moving oxen team.

A streak of light flashed across the space from one of the figures and hit the rear panel, blasting a chunk of wood off of it. It left a fist sized indention glowing like fresh snow in the moonlight. Barney hurled the bag out of the back and watched as it crashed to the snow. He waited for a moment, letting their pursuers get closer and closer. Finally, just as they reached it, he hurled a ball of fire across the snowy courtyard. It streaked through the morning haze and crashed over the sack like a bottle breaking across an unsuspecting man's head, sending little streaks of fire spitting off in every direction and sizzling in the snow. The bag caught fire instantly and burned for a fraction of a breath. Then it erupted.

An explosion ripped into the darkness and snow. A plume of fire and smoke burst out in every direction, accompanied by a deafening roar that left all their ears ringing. It lit the entire courtyard up like full day for the blink of an eye before receding and leaving them all half-blind. A cascade of smoking stones and debris sailed across the yard with the wave of heat that hit them, crashing into the snow like falling stars in every direction. Taron saw that all the mages that had been following were thrown down, either motionless shapes in the snow or little pyres burning close to the crater left by the explosion. Barney gave him a wild grin, a slightly manic look in his eye.

"Nothing like a little blasting powder to even the odds, eh?"

Taron nodded wordlessly. He moved back to the front of the wagon and that was when he saw the gate. It was closed and barred, with a contingent of robed figures blocking the way. At the head of the figures was the bearded, burly Castellan, the mage Roegan. He stepped forward and lifted his hands, face fixed in a grimace that was equal parts fury and effort. The ground before him rose like a wave with a gargantuan groan, building up into a great torrent of earth that threatened to swallow them up. Holton turned the oxen hard, the wagon skidding and sliding up on two wheels as it fought to keep up. Barney and Taron instinctively threw themselves to the floor on the opposite side.

Their weight brought it crashing back down with a bone rattling thud. For a moment, they seemed not to be moving at all. Then the wagon slung them backwards as it was yanked straight by the oxen. The younger man nearly tumbled out of the back but Taron was able to grab him by the collar of his coat and haul him back into the wagon. As they sat beside each other, they could see the wave of stone and dirt and snow bearing down on them, casting them in a shadow that blotted out the little bit of orange light that had managed to creep across the sky. The sound was deafening, a grinding roar of stone on stone like a ceaseless avalanche. Taron reached over and grabbed the second sack.

"We need that to blow the gate!" Barney screamed at him.

"It won't matter if we're buried alive!" He yelled back and stood, shakily trying to maintain his footing in the wagon as it pitched back and forth. He glanced at Barney and hefted the sack out the back with all his strength, throwing it as high as he could.

In his weakened state, Taron barely managed to get it much above the roof line of the wagon. But as it met with the wall of debris that was almost upon them, Barney hurled another ball of fire after it. As the red ball met the cloth it instantly ignited, flowering out over the surface for a fraction of a moment before the explosion. Even as the wagon moved away, the blast was far too close this time. The heat from it burned the exposed skin on his face and hands. It knocked both men backwards with its concussive heatwave. The entire wagon was put off balance, wildly weaving back and forth behind the charging oxen.

Through ringing in his ears, Taron could hear Holton cursing up front as he fought to maintain control of the panicked animals. His vision was all spots and halos, but he could make out the flaming wreckage of the earthen wave raining down all around them. A great deal of it struck the wagon, but the blast had broken it up enough that the debris slid off the roof harmlessly. He checked to see that Barney was still groaning beside him before turning and crawling up towards the front once more. Holton and Erin had managed to wrangle control of the hairy beasts once again, and now had the wagon retracing its path back towards the stables.

"That gate's a no go. We'll have to go with the last resort." Taron yelled out to them.

"Do you think it'll be enough?" Erin cried back over the wind and the residual clamor of debris still raining down.

"It's going to have to be. Get the kid!" Holton ordered.

Taron nodded and shuffled back into the wagon. Barney had pushed himself up into a sitting position. He was moving his jaw back and forth like it was causing him great pain. Taron got his attention.

"You're up, kid. This is our last shot to get out of here."

Barney looked up at him, struck dumb for a moment. Then he seemed to understand what the older Northman was saying and nodded, a grim look on his face. He reached over and grabbed the crossbow he had dropped during the confusion and handed it to Taron. Then he stood and moved towards the front of the wagon, swapping out with Erin on the driver seat. As the woman moved back beside Taron, her crossbow held at the ready, their eyes met and they exchanged silent recognition.

"These things are a godsend." She remarked, indicating the crossbow in her hands, "And you thought they were too expensive."

Taron snorted, "We can talk numbers once we get out of here."

"Here they come." Erin said, her voice sounding exhausted but full of grit. They hefted their weapons to their shoulders and took aim out the back door.

Several cloaked figures were in pursuit again, gliding over the snow with supernatural speed, gracefully weaving between the hunks of smoking earth that now littered the courtyard. Erin sent a bolt flying towards the closest of them, but it sailed just to its right and disappeared into the early morning gloom. Taron did his best to keep the crossbow steady despite his still shaking hands and pulled the trigger. It kicked as the bolt shot out and struck one of the pursuers in the shoulder. He grinned and turned to check on their progress. The sun had risen higher and he could see the outline of the stable sprawling against the base of the far wall, even at their distance. He saw Barney moving to readjust, another ball of fire already glowing in his hand. They were closing on the stable quickly, already passing the crater and the charred remains of their earlier encounter.

He heard Holton lean in and ask, "How close do you need to get?"

"Just a little closer..." He heard Barney mutter.

In the young man's hand, the fiery globe grew larger and larger until it was like a torch, spitting tongues of fire and sizzling in the icy wind. Taron could feel the heat radiating off of it. Barney stood and turned his body, readying to hurl the flaming ball at the last of their wagons. But then the world was turned upside down. A sound like thunder rocked their bodies and the wagon lurched forward. Taron smashed his face into the back of the driver's seat, the taste of blood immediately filling his mouth. White hot pain flashed across his face. He cursed and fought the gathering blackness in his vision to stay awake. He shook his head to try and clear it and looked around, desperately trying to get his bearings.

Holton and Barney had been thrown forward, off the driver's seat, disappearing out front of the cart somewhere. Taron turned and saw Erin lying on the floor of the wagon, groaning and nearly unconscious herself, face a bloodied mess from where she had slammed into the wagon. He moved back and gathered her up, growling at her to stay awake as he hauled her out the front with one hand while carrying his crossbow with the other. He managed to get her out onto the driver's seat, where he stood up to survey the damage.

Barney had smashed into the snow a few paces out and Holton had landed on the back of one of the oxen, who were all bellowing in pain and frustration after being violently jerked to a stop. Barney had dropped his ball of fire and it must have burst on the ground where it landed. There was a circle of melted snow and the wheel of the wagon was engulfed in flames. From his vantage point, he could see that stone spikes had erupted from the ground and skewered the wheels of the wagon like a dozen blackened blades. They jutted out in every direction like a wicked, overgrown hedge.

He cursed and fumbled with his crossbow as he checked behind them. A contingent of cloaked figures was advancing on them, led by the unmistakable rotund form of Roegan. To his dismay, Taron could see these were not all brown cloaked apprentices. Many wore shades of gray and black, some walking with staves or rods in hand. Taron cursed again and hefted his crossbow, using the roof beam of the wagon as a bracing stand. The smoke made his eyes sting, but he ignored it and sent a bolt flying at the fat old wizard.

The bolt flew true but it hit something invisible about five paces from the mage, splintering apart in midair. Taron cursed for a third time, reloaded and shot again. He yelled to his compatriots, but they were all groaning and struggling against unconsciousness. Taron cast his gaze about wildly as he pulled the reloading lever, hearing the mechanism click into place inside the weapon. He loaded a second bolt and took aim. The mages were not far now and were closing quickly.

The bearded Northman readjusted and sent another bolt at the mage to Roegan's right, but it burst against the invisible barrier and fell to the ground harmlessly just like the first. Taron screamed at Holton and Erin as he fumbled with his second to last bolt, begging them to get up. He took aim at the mage to the left of the Castellan this time, hoping to find some hole in their defense. He was preparing to pull the trigger when a new sound drew his attention.

At first, he thought it was another eruption of the earth. But then he turned his head and saw dozens of shapes headed towards them. In the low light it took him a moment to figure out what he was seeing. But soon, a stampede of oxen and cattle and horses and goats materialized out of the gloom, all beasts from the stable. They thundered past, flowing around the cart like a river being split by a stone. Taron watched as the herd charged into the mages, barely hindered as they rammed into whatever invisible shield they had constructed. The first few of the beasts were stopped in their tracks, but they were slammed into by the rest of the animals and forced through it. Some tried to turn and run, but it happened too quickly. The mages screamed as they were swallowed up by a flurry of hooves and fur, disappearing beneath the herd.

Taron watched in morbid fascination until he remembered his compatriots. He spun around and saw that Barney had recovered enough of his wits to crawl under the wagon to protect himself as the beasts ran by. Holton was watching the spectacle from the back of one of the oxen, mouth agape as he stared around at the sight. Erin was still groaning, eyes closed as she lay on the driver's seat. Looking up, Taron saw that behind the herd, another shape was jostling along. It was the second of their wagons, being drawn by the two oxen they had left behind. At the reins was Jarryd, a bloodied mess with clothes torn and wounds across his body. But as he pulled the cart to a stop beside their own, he leapt to his feet and motioned towards Taron.

"Help me get the others on board!"

"Jarryd! Where did *you* come from?" The Northman asked as he gathered up Erin and began the process of carrying her to the other cart.

Jarryd leapt down and began helping Barney to his feet, "A mage helped me find the way out, a woman with dark hair. I was saddling up the second wagon to catch up with you when I heard the explosion and saw you headed back this way. Released all the animals and spooked them with a bit of blasting powder so they'd charge. Get ready, the fire should reach the last cart any moment now."

"The fire-" Taron looked and realized smoke was pluming out through all the windows of the stable.

The third explosion hit them, cutting him off mid sentence. He had thought the previous explosions were loud, but this rocked Taron to his very core. He felt like it kicked at his guts from the inside, a massive wave of air and heat that knocked the wind out of him and left him gasping. It was deafening, so loud he thought it might knock his teeth loose. After, he could not even hear the wind howling around them. As the fiery blast shook the earth and ripped the stable to pieces, it sent a pillar of mingled red and black erupting into the sky as tall as the castle's highest tower. The sky lit up in a brilliant corona of orange and yellow, leaving them all fighting to recover their vision. Jets of fire and massive hunks of stone and lumber tumbled through the air in every direction, crashing to earth like falling stars and smoldering in the snow.

The smoking ruin left behind was unrecognizable as a stable, only a loose assortment of rubble. But it was what lay beyond that caught Taron's eye. The wall, which the stable had been at the base of, was now run through with a network of cracks that radiated outward from the explosion's point of origin. Like a great spiderweb they decorated the wall's surface, leaving the once imposing visage pockmarked and crumbling. Taron could not see the bottom, as it was still shrouded in smoke and fire, but he thought he could glimpse the barest hint of light there.

Once they were able to get the rest of their crew loaded into the last of the carts they had brought up here, Jarryd resumed his place at the reins while Taron recovered his crossbow and sat beside him. He glanced back towards the large herd of animals, now milling about in the courtyard. His ears still rang and he felt wheezy and exhausted, but he saw that there was a form moving among the beasts. The stout figure of Roegan stumbled up to his feet, sloughing off hunks of stone and dirt. He was surveying the scene around him, not looking their way yet.

Taron stared for a moment, amazed the grizzled old mage had had the wit to shield himself from the stampede in time. But his hesitation lasted barely a moment. He lifted his weapon to his shoulder, aimed and pulled the trigger. The bolt flew true, smacking into the mage's shoulder and earning a shriek of surprise as he fell to the ground. The sound startled the creatures around him and they began to kick and stomp at the man. Taron imagined they must have thought he was a predator lurking in their midst. He did not see what was left of the mage, but the portly man did not rise again.

Jarryd had brought the cart to a rattling start by the time Taron turned back around. They rode in silence towards the wreckage of the stables, letting their senses recover. Once they reached the wall, they could just see that there was a crack in it large enough to see pale light on the other side. They both leapt down and began the process of clearing rubble from the wagon's path.

"I suppose it's a good thing we filled that wagon to the brim with blasting powder." Taron commented wryly.

"Aye. Any less and we would be stuck waiting on the mages like foxes cornered by hounds." Jarryd agreed.

By the time they reached the hole in the wall, they could hear voices yelling in confusion. Through the haze and winds, they could just make out more cloaked figures spilling out of the castle and into the courtyard. Taron let out a frustrated grunt as they hurried to cajole the two remaining oxen through the wall. It took no small effort, the beasts were reluctant to move through the smoke and smoldering wreckage. But they were helped along by Holton as he sat in the driver's seat and spoke to them in a low, soothing voice. Somewhere behind them, the mages were moving closer, to inspect what was left of the stable. They had not yet seen the thieves among the chaos and the snowstorm, but they would soon enough.

The wall had been several feet thick of layered stone and the blast had barely made a hole big enough for them to squeeze the wagon through. It was slow going over the uneven ground and by the time they were halfway through the hole, they could clearly hear the voices behind them.

"Search every inch of the wreckage!" They heard someone yell out, "Those bastards might be hiding in there!"

The crew exchanged haggard looks. Their faces were drawn in exhaustion and pain, none ready for another fight. Holton took a long, ragged breath and reached to grab his hatchet in his good hand, when they heard screaming of a different kind. It was high pitched and panicky, a woman's voice from far behind them, somewhere in the direction of the castle.

"The wall!" She cried, "Down below! The wall is cracking!"

Immediately, yells of surprise and alarm followed the woman's pronouncement. They could hear the sounds of men calling out the alarm and turning to run back away from the wreckage. They did not hesitate, but pushed on as fast as they could until they managed to force the wagon through the narrow crevice.

It was full day when the crew emerged on the other side of the wall, stumbling into the barren tundra of the Far North once again. The light served to further illustrate the stark landscape around them. Jarryd gracefully maneuvered himself up onto the driver's seat beside Holton while Taron slung himself up into the bed beside the two others. He sat staring out the back as the wagon rolled out through the fresh snow, watching as the black castle slowly grew smaller and smaller in the distance. The wind blustered and beat at the wagon as they rolled across the open fjord, back towards the south, away from the dark castle at the edge of the earth.

Chapter Ten

The Wizard

The wind was howling through the pines, carrying a chill that cut straight to the bone. A storm was coming, less than a day away. Holton knew it as surely as he did his own face in the mirror. He could scent it on the air, knew it was going to be the kind that lashed at the North like a cruel cattle driver. As he stalked through the heavy snow, the new fall quickly filling the footprints he left in his wake, Holton considered the impending storm a good fortune. They seemed to have left the mages far behind, losing whatever trackers were following them on the long trek across the frozen tundra, but he knew better than to assume safety just because of a little distance. He welcomed anything that would help hide their trail and harry any pursuers. He knew he would likely not sleep easy until they were three kingdoms away from Coldwater, at the least.

As he moved further into the forest, away from the dingy roadside inn where his crew had taken up shelter for the night, he listened and scanned the treeline all around. Whatever gods truly presided over this world, whether it was the Elders of the Northern Tribes, the Southerners Pantheon, the One True God of the Empire or some other, stranger deity he was unfamiliar with, they had blessed him with keen ears and sharp eyes. But the quarry he sought tonight was a tricky one, and Holton was no fan of being caught unaware.

Suddenly, up ahead of him a short distance, a gray coated figure appeared out of the darkness. He did not walk into Holton's field of vision, nor did he step out from behind some tree or other cover. The yellow face of the full moon cast its glow so strongly across the forest that he was certain. One moment there was nothing but empty forest before him, then the figure just appeared out of the air like a dread specter. Only the snow settling on his shoulders and hood made it clear he was there in truth and not some ghostly image.

But Holton was undeterred by the figure's sudden appearance, trudging along until he was a few paces away. Beneath the hood, he could see the man's sharp featured face framed by long dark hair and sly grin likewise framed by a pointed beard. The man wore a fine, waxed overcoat which was lined in dark fur and looked like it cost enough to feed a family for an entire season. Holton stood in silence, waiting as the wind filled the space between himself and the well dressed man. Finally, grin slipping a bit, the man shifted his weight and spoke up.

"I see you made it out of Coldwater alive." His voice was smooth like sweet honey wine from the Southlands. To Holton, it sounded too soft.

The red haired thief nodded, "By the skin of our teeth. Did you come out here from the inn for our meeting?"

"No, no, my camp is back that way." He motioned over his shoulder, "I'd not stay in any public establishments right now. It would be very complicated if I was known to be here, even by rumor."

"Because of all those big plans you won't tell me about?" Holton pried, an edge creeping into his voice.

The black haired man showed his teeth, "Now Holton, we don't know each other that well quite yet."

"We don't know each other at all." Holton unhooked a loop that held his great overcoat shut and dug inside, suddenly feeling the cold sharp against his skin through the layers of cloth underneath. He found the Glass and brought it out, holding it up so the Wizard could see. It was so clear it would have been nearly invisible in the low light if not for the thin silver ring around it, "But I'd say we're damn near like brothers after this job. Me and my crew nearly died for this trinket of yours."

The man's dark eyes fixed on the Glass. They gleamed in the moonlight like deep, still pools. He held out a hand, "Excellent work, Holton. You've surpassed all my expectations."

But the red haired thief pulled the Glass back, cradling it close to his chest. The grin slipped from the mage's face for the first time, curling into a slight frown. He shifted his weight and spoke with a slight trace of annoyance in his tone.

"You have issues with our deal...?"

"The deal was to steal the Glass from the College," Holton said, tone still carrying that edge of annoyance, "but you didn't tell us everything."

"I told you there would be resistance."

Holton snorted, "You didn't mention the monsters."

"It changes nothing."

"Like hell it doesn't." The thief nodded down to the Glass, "What are you going to use this for? Are you calling down those creatures on the people of the North?"

It was the Wizard's turn to snort, waving a dismissive hand, "Our plans are far greater than that."

"What then? What exactly do you intend to do with this thing?"

"Did the old woman tell you what the Glass does?"

"We never got to that. I know it let her speak with those creatures."

"It does much more than that. Quentin Cross was a visionary mage, one of the most gifted of his generation, but he was shortsighted." The dark haired man shook his head, "He made the Glass to help facilitate communication with beings like the ones you saw, but he failed to fully grasp the potential of what it could do."

"Which is?"

"The Glass doesn't translate language, it converts energy. The creatures you saw at Coldwater are ancient, with a lineage that dates back to the very creation of the world. Some arcanists refer to their kind as Primals. Creatures such as those use what you and I bend magic instinctively, without need for spellwork or rituals. The creatures don't communicate with each other through speech as you and I understand it, they use magic. What we hear, that strange song, is only the echoes of that." His tone had gotten more excited the longer he spoke. There was an unsettling edge to it.

Holton thought back to the chamber with the ice wall, about how he had heard the creatures. How their speech had seemed to cut straight through him, to reverberate through his entire body. Like a wave of cold that sapped every drop of strength from him and left him cold. It set his teeth on edge. He shook himself, suddenly aware that he had been silent for a long moment, "So what would you need a tool like that for? The Keeper said you were building something."

The dark haired man's eyes narrowed, "Indeed. My compatriots are building a machine, an endeavor that will be greatly expedited by the use of that Glass. We would need years to fabricate a device of similar capability."

Holton considered this for a moment. The wind was still billowing around them, tugging at their greatcoats and tossing icy flurries of white back and forth across the space between them. All around, it seemed to Holton the forest seemed to have grown darker in the short while they had been speaking, darker and colder. He turned the Glass over in his hand as he pondered the mage's words.

"And Aurelia...she disagreed with your plans?"

The Wizard sighed, "What we aim to do...it's quite ambitious. Not everyone has the stomach for that sort of thing."

"But the other mage, the dark haired woman, she does?" Holton eyed the man closely, "You never mentioned her before, how does she figure into your schemes?"

"When my meeting with the Keeper went...*poorly*, Cassandra reached out to me." His lip curled into a sly smile, "She was the old woman's second in command, she was there for our meeting. She saw the potential in our plans and she was quite ready to step out from her mentor's shadow."

"When we last met, before the job, you said these plans of yours were going to change the world, topple kingdoms..."

He nodded, eyes fixed on the Glass. Holton noted the greedy shine in the man's eyes and kept turning the bauble, speaking low, choosing his words carefully, "...you said there would be opportunities for those who chose to take them."

"I did..."

"After this job, this job that *you* sent my crew and I on, we are going to need a safe place to go, somewhere far and safe from the College. So I'm choosing to take one of those opportunities."

The mage blinked and looked up, staring silently at Holton for a moment as though he had forgotten the other man was there. That insufferable sly smile slowly slithered back across his lips and he said, "You have proven to be quite useful, and we may need your services in the future, Holton. But you're in no position to make demands."

"Aren't I? I have the Glass."

"You think I couldn't take it from you if I chose to?" The Wizard still smiled, but there was an unmistakable hard edge to his tone now. It might have been Holton's imagination, but the air around the mage seemed to warble and blur as though it were a particularly hot day.

"You could try." Holton cast an eye towards the trees encircling them.

Shapes emerged from the darkness. They were large, shambling shadows that moved closer from out of the surrounding blackness. Soon though, it became easier to see their smashed faces with their short snouts jutting out over snarling jaws full of sharp teeth. Their thick, matted fur was peppered with white flurries and ice, frozen clumps hanging from their long arms and backs. They stopped a few paces from the men, forming a loose circle as they watched the men with dark, malicious eyes that glimmered with hunger. The Wizard watched the creatures approaching with a cautious, appraising eye. Even in the cold and the strong crosswind, the creatures stank of gore and filth. The mage raised an eyebrow at the thief.

"You can control them?"

"Not so much. But winter is a tough season for the wyler-beasts." Holton replied, "It was easy to persuade them to follow me with the promise of fresh meat."

"You're more powerful than most Speakers I've known. Most of them can barely communicate with one or two types of beast. This borders on the High Art."

"I've had a great deal of practice." He replied, shrugging off the compliment, "It's amazing what you find you can do when your life depends on it again and again."

The mage nodded. His grin had disappeared again and he stood uneasily, eyes roaming back and forth across the circle of creatures. He forced himself to meet the thief's gaze, "You are more resourceful than I thought. Perhaps I can find a place for you in our greater plans after all."

"What sort of place? Speak plainly, I've had enough of these games."

"I can't tell you everything, too much risk if you were to get caught and put to the rack. But I can tell you our operation is moving into the New World."

"Loraillia?"

The Wizard nodded, "Things there are still unstable. Ever since the Federation's colonies declared independence, the New World has become a powder keg. Over two decades of conflict with everyone trying to stake their claim and carve out a piece for themselves."

"You're talking about the Free Cities?"

"Yes, but not just them; New Oarenhiem and the uncharted lands beyond as well. The New World is vast and we've only uncovered a fraction of what it has to offer. If even some of the rumors of what the Scivian Empire has found in the south are to be believed..."

But Holton cut him off, "You're offering to take me and my crew to the New World?"

"I'm offering to *discuss* it with you, if you continue to be useful. We have a distance to go before we enact our plans. Many more jobs across the North, and the rest of Evardene. But, I think a man as capable as you could cut yourself out a nice little life in the New World if all goes according to plan."

Holton thought about this for a moment. He had been born in the North, lived here all his life. The cold and the snow and the evergreen trees were all he knew. But the North was also where he had made his reputation. The Red Wolf was well known, and his reputation was only going to keep growing, especially after this last job. He cast a glance back towards the inn. It was lost in the dark now, soft lights swallowed up in the cold night.

"We can change your life, Holton. Save it, from those that would have your head on a pike. Yours and all of your men. But it all starts with you giving me that Glass."

The mage held out a hand shod in soft black leather. Holton watched as delicate white spots clung to the glove despite the harsh winds. He turned the disk of glass and metal over in his hand once more, feeling as though it suddenly weighed a great deal more than only a moment before. Then he set it in the mage's hand. The Wizard's grin returned and he nodded, quickly tucking the Glass away inside his own coat. Holton was confused as he pulled his hand out, thinking for a moment he still had the Glass in his hand. But then he saw the famil-iar metallic glint came instead from a large coin the mage had produced. As he held it up, Holton could see it held a blade engulfed in flame emblazoned on its face.

"Consider this my token," the mage told him formally, as though he were bestowing Holton with a great gift, "and an official mark of your association with the Burning Blades."

Holton gazed down at the coin. He flipped it over to see the elaborately engraved double B's entwined on its opposite face. He stuffed the coin inside his jacket and buttoned it against the cold. When he looked up, the Wizard was still staring at him.

"Are you going to call off these beasts?"

He looked around at the pack of monsters. He had been projecting out a feeling of calm since they arrived, to ensure they did not pounce on the mage prematurely. It was easy work for him. He had learned to do it years before, as a child, when he had minded the mules and goats on his family farm. He changed his focus, looking around at each of the beasts in turn. They regarded him for a moment, then turned back towards the direction he had come from. They stalked back into the darkness in a group, moving with a sort of lumbering gait as their long arms swung at their sides. Before long, the creatures were gone, leaving the thief and the mage alone once again.

"Where ever did you find those creatures?" The dark haired man asked, his tone lighter, slightly amused even, now that the monsters were gone.

Holton was still watching the darkness after them, "There are many wyler packs here in the Far North. They've been pushed out by men, to the farthest places, and this deep into winter, they're getting desperate. They don't stay as far from humans as they should, scavenging and killing off livestock when they can."

"Then how did you get them to leave?"

"I gave them the image of a dead oxen carcass in the smoke-house outside the inn. An easy meal."

"Is there?" The mage arched an eyebrow.

"You can't lie when you're Speaking to an animal."

"Oh no?"

Holton shook his head, "It's not like with us. It's more dire ct...simpler."

"Much like how the Primals communicate, I would imagine?"

Holton's gaze snapped up and he caught the mage's eye, "What do you know of it?"

"Little, only what I've read in old accounts and journals." The Wizard shrugged, "But from what I know, it's quite something to interact with one directly. There are rumors of men being driven mad from such encounters."

He looked meaningfully at the thief. Holton held his gaze, defiant in the face of his questioning. The dark haired man gave a dismissive gesture, "I wouldn't put too much stock in such things. They're likely old wives tales, meant to scare children."

He turned to go but Holton called out, "If we're going to be working together, I think I should know your name."

The Wizard stared off into the trees, his eyes taking on a glint that was unsettling. The grin had disappeared again, leaving his face notably harder. It occurred to Holton in that moment the man might have been considerably older than he appeared underneath the expensive clothing and fine grooming. He spoke without looking at the red haired thief, tone low and flat.

"I have had many names," he said, voice so low Holton had to strain his ears to hear, "but most call me Lawrence these days."

For a moment, both men were silent. Lawrence blinked a few times, as though the wind were bothering him. Then he took a deep breath and the grin wormed its way across his face for a final time as he looked up to face Holton once again, "Time to go, my friend."

"We are no friends to each other, mage. Perhaps once you get my crew and I to the New World we can share a flagon of ale."

Lawrence nodded and turned away, beginning his trek back into the woods toward his unseen camp. Before he was swallowed by the night, he called back over his shoulder, "Keep that coin handy. I'll be calling for you with your next assignment soon."

Holton watched until he disappeared, seemingly leaving the thief alone in the empty forest. But the red haired man knew he was not alone. With the senses of a Speaker, he could reach out and feel the small family of white foxes curled beneath a tree ten paces to his right. He could sense the great snowy owl that watched him from above in the canopy, its golden eyes luminescent against the dark. He could feel the jubilation of the wylerbeasts at having uncovered the dead oxen, a victim of their hard push across the tundra on their flight from Coldwater. They had drug it into the forest and were now ripping it apart in a frenzy, simple minds absorbed totally in their meal.

He pulled his coat tight around himself and turned to trudge back through the woods towards the inn and the rest of his crew. He could sense them too, like little sparks of light flickering in the rapidly worsening storm. He hurried his pace as he moved towards them, ready to be out of the foul weather.

The End

The Coldwater Job
A Crucible of Legacy Novella

DEAR READER

To all those readers who chose to give this book a chance, to pick it up off the shelf or download it on your device, I want to take a moment to say a heartfelt thank you. I have loved stories and storytelling since I was a child, and it has always been my dream to write novels of my very own. I have spent so much time and poured so much of myself into the process of making this series a reality. But in truth, writing the book is only half the battle. It is you, the readers, that make or break every book. You determine if a book will be a success, and your support and recommendations are what drive the career of every successful author. Without you, none of this would be possible. So again, I say thank you. Just by reading this book, you are helping me achieve a dream I have had since I was a kid.

Be assured, it is my intention to keep writing, to finish this series and see these character's stories through to their conclusions. I hope that you have enjoyed my work so far and will continue this journey with me. If so, I want ask you one more favor. Please consider rating and reviewing *The Coldwater Job* on Amazon and any other book related sites you might use. Ratings and reviews are the lifeblood that keep books relevant and help them stand out in a competitive and ever growing market. Your reviews directly support my work and might be the thing that convinces others to give this book a shot. Hopefully, with your support, I can keep growing this passion project of mine and get my work into the hands of many more readers just like you.

If you enjoyed this novella, the story continues with the next installment in the Crucible of Legacy series, *The Scion Conspiracy*, available everywhere books are sold.

For those who have made it this far, thank you so much for your support, your time and your belief in me.

Sincerely,
Mike Cahoon

ABOUT THE AUTHOR

Mike Cahoon is an independent author with a deep love of stories across many genres and mediums, but he always holds a special place in his heart for his personal holy trinity of fantasy, science fiction and horror. Growing up, he was a terrible student despite his teacher's and parent's best attempts to get him to apply himself. Despite this, he had a passion for reading and writing which has stubbornly stuck with him throughout his entire life. Now he is finally embarking on his own literary journey and getting the stories out of his head that have been knocking around in there for decades.

Born and raised in Atlanta, Mike has spent most of his adult life as a firefighter in his community. He still resides in the metro area where he lives the suburban life with his wife, two daughters and their great, big dog. When he's not writing, he enjoys anything outside, cooking for his family, being exceedingly okay at jiu jitsu and drinking too much coffee.

If you would like to keep up with Mike and get updates on his various projects, sign up for his newsletter on mikecahoon.com and be sure to follow him on social media @mikecahoon_author.